Homo intellectus

James Anthony

Published by YouWriteOn.com, 2011

First Edition

British Library C.I.P.

A CIP catalogue record for this title is available from the British Library.

ISBN

978-1-908481-55-9

With thanks to my wife,
without whose encouragement and endless support,
I could not have created this story.

"The world was once a featureless place. None of the places we know existed until creator beings, in the forms of people, plants and animals, travelled widely across the land.

Then, in a process of creation and destruction, they formed the landscape as we know it today. Anangu land is still inhabited by the spirits of dozens of these ancestral creator beings which are referred to as Tjukuritja or Waparitja."

Commonwealth Department of Environment's
Uluru Web page
Retrieved 8th April 2010

Prologue

What is now the Sahara desert - 92,453 BCE

Lucere closed his eyes and waited. Years of difficulties had led to this point, many failures and many lives. It was imperative this time they had resolved all of the problems.

Orcanna gave the instruction for the stone cover to be removed. A surge of overwhelming energy coursed through Lucere's fragile body. A blinding light of pure white exploded behind his eyelids. Physical sensations, the cold of the stone in which he lay, the hum of the power source, the scents of the carefully formulated body oils, all faded as he felt himself projected into a swirling tunnel of brilliant patterns. Faster and faster the images swallowed him until he started to feel totally disoriented.

In the distance a small black dot, closer and closer. Perhaps this is the end? Perhaps what they'd discovered, what they'd worked for could not be achieved?

Suddenly, he burst through the darkness. His body lay motionless beneath. The glow from the crystal touching his head faded. He watched Orcanna lean forward and touch his chest, feeling for signs of life. Orcanna stood back and shook his head.

Lucere had to find a way to communicate. It had worked! They had finally achieved their objective. Now, many Orbiannes would be able to follow. But how could he communicate?

He focused on Orcanna and projected the words, 'success ... success'. Orcanna looked about the circular room, but no-one was there. He raised his eyes. A small ball of light hovered near the ceiling of the stone room. Orcanna nodded and smiled. He hurried from the chamber to start the long process of transforming what remained of the population.

Chapter One

Los Angeles
Thursday 12th April 2029

"Right, Cartwright, what should I tell the President! I've got a call with him in an hour and he's not happy. Billions of dollars have been spent funding NASA and when it comes to the crunch we failed ... failed badly." The Administrator of NASA, Chuck Greenburn, was visibly shaken. He'd been fending off calls for the last two days from staff and press alike.

"Well sir, to be honest, we've no idea what's gone wrong. The Asteroid's been monitored continuously since it was identified by the Kitts Peak Observatory in June 2004 and although we knew it was predicted to pass very close to earth tomorrow, we have no idea how it changed orbit to a collision course!" Professor Simon Cartwright, Si to his friends, had worked at NASA for the last ten years on the Near Earth Objects programme that monitored small bodies in our solar system. "We're now certain of the impact area, it may not be as catastrophic as we think. It's currently predicted to impact into North Africa, the middle of the Sahara." Si reported the latest predictions, although following recent events, he wouldn't stake his life on anything right now.

"Even the missile we sent didn't have any effect, have they found out what happened yet?" Greenburn demanded.

"It's not really my field, sir, but, from what I understand, they lost contact with the Command Control computer when it approached the asteroid. Even the targeting radar system didn't detonate the warhead, it exploded thousands of kilometres away." Si couldn't believe what had happened either. The missile had been developed for just such a mission. Previous tests on smaller asteroids had been perfect. Now it was too late to send another, the detonation would be too close to earth and would irradiate half the planet.

"So you're saying I should tell the President that we have no idea what's going to happen ... sorry!" shouted Greenburn.

"Sir, I'm a scientist, diplomacy isn't my strong point. All we know is that it could be a lot worse." Si reported the latest predictions, although following recent events, he wouldn't stake his life on anything right now.

"Great! OK Cartwright, get out. If anything develops, let me know immediately." Greenburn turned to his communications console with a worried look.

Si left the office and headed back to the Jet Propulsion Laboratories where, now aged 46, he'd spent most of his last ten years. When he was offered a position in the Near Earth Objects team in Pasadena, following his Thesis on 'Object Tracking in Deep Space', he was over the moon. Unfortunately, his wife Sally, didn't share his enthusiasm for the States. '*So I'll be left bringing up Ben and Abigail in a country I don't like while you play scientist. Sorry Si, I think we've come to the end of the road.*'

In reality, she was acknowledging something they had both been ignoring for some time. They just didn't get on any more. Something had slipped away when they weren't looking and they were leading separate lives, Si immersed in

Astrophysics and Sally bringing up two young children on her own.

Si, now recognised as a world expert on Asteroids, Meteors and their trajectories, worked with his team to study threats and plot their courses to identify any danger to Earth.

He entered the main office and glanced at the large display panel on the wall. The current predicted path of the earth and asteroid 99942 moved slowly together in time to a digital display set to Greenwich Mean Time in the corner of the screen. The count down clock ticked away, one day, three hours, fourteen minutes. The Asteroid had been named Apophis by the scientists that discovered it, appropriately after the Egyptian god of evil and destruction who dwelt in eternal darkness.

Robin was sitting at the main control panel.

"Any new developments?" Si shouted as he crossed the cluttered room full of computers, cables and RAID discs.

"We've had a call from SETI, the Search For Extra-Terrestrial Intelligence people. They got some strange readings on their equipment a month ago at the same time the Asteroid changed direction," Robin explained. "It seems a large electromagnetic pulse appeared next to the Asteroid and deflected its course. They've been checking and re-checking everything looking for a reason, but they haven't got any explanation, it's a complete mystery."

"Another one," mused Si, half absorbed in thought.

He re-crossed the cluttered floor to his office to get some peace and quiet to think. Could Newton and Einstein be wrong? Maybe there is something else out there beyond our current understanding. We know at the sub-atomic level their laws don't work too well, maybe there's also a flaw at the stella level we haven't discovered yet?

He thought back to the events of the previous months. Since the shift in orbit, the world had reacted in different ways. Panic had set in on the world stock markets causing economic disasters to some countries, similar to the problems caused by the World's Banking system collapse in 2008.

Marches had been held in various cities across the globe with people demanding action following the failure of the deflection missile.

Various mainstream religious organisations took it as a sign from God for humanity to mend its ways. *Our modern day Sodom and Gomorrah.*

Some of the fringe cults planned to assemble on various points of high ground to commune with the asteroid as it passed overhead.

For a while things had settled down following the prediction that the target area for the asteroid was North Africa. The Governments in Mali and the surrounding countries were offered help to move their populations, but the problems of assembling their people, who lived in small communities across vast expanses of desert, was deemed too difficult.

Strangely, the people in the target area around Timbuktu were welcoming the asteroid as an event long forecast in their myths and legends. The event was even depicted in thirty thousand year old cave art in both northern and southern Africa.

He pulled his mind back into focus, it was seven in the evening and there was nothing more he could do tonight. He'd been at the office for the last forty eight hours straight, so he left instructions to call if anything changed, and went home to try and get some sleep.

Chapter Two

Friday 13th April 2029

After a restless night where apocalyptic visions of devastation had haunted him, Si woke early. He showered, dressed and gulped down a mug of tea, his favourite brand sent to him by his ex-wife along with a few photo's of their children from the school Christmas Nativity play.

Out of the apartment and into his sixty year old classic Jaguar Mk2 3.4 litre. A frivolous expense that kept him grounded in the UK. He joined the early morning traffic and headed for Oak Grove Drive. Right-hand drive didn't seem to present a problem in the States, wide lanes and overtaking either side solved most of the problems. Not the same as when they used to drive through France on their way to holiday on the Italian Riviera.

The drive wasn't long, he'd been lucky renting a small house on the estate near to his office at the Jet Propulsion Laboratory.

Twenty minutes later he was re-entering the control room. A glance at the screen confirmed nothing had changed. The predicted landfall for the asteroid was now confirmed as the Sahara, a few hundred miles north of Timbuktu.

The countdown was showing seven hours, twelve minutes to impact. Images from an orbiting satellite filled another screen showing the asteroid, a craggy lump of rock nearly 400 metres across, glinting in the sunlight as it slowly grew larger.

Travelling with an approach speed of more than eighteen thousand kilometres an hour and accelerating as the earth's gravity took hold. It wasn't going to wipe out the planet, the impact was estimated at 500 megatons, but the consequences of its impact were uncertain. We hadn't had an impact this size in recorded memory. The last impact in 1908, the Tunguska event over Russia, was only a few metres across and had burst in the air before impact.

Si knew that underneath the predicted impact zone of this asteroid was a large magma dome that had been lifting parts of Africa for hundreds of thousands of years. Could the impact rupture the earth's crust and release the molten lava? Could shock-waves reach the Mediterranean and cause a tsunami which would devastate coastal areas in the land-locked sea? All of these scenarios and many others were possible.

A corner of the display screen was occupied by a national news channel, currently showing a panel of 'experts', discussing the various possibilities. Of course, the truth was no one had any idea. It wouldn't be long before they would all know. Air travel had been reduced to a few essential movements, many people had been given the day off work. Some of these were gathered in public spaces all over the world where large television screens had been erected. They flipped between various discussions of the asteroid and satellite images of the predicted impact area in the Sahara desert.

Si went into his office to check his emails, nothing new since last night. He glanced through his office window, the countdown read six hours, thirty two minutes. He wandered out into the main office to check with Robin if the impact location had changed overnight.

"Si, I can hear your cellphone ringing." Claire shouted across the noisy computer filled room.

"Can you pick it up, might be my ex-wife, it's somewhere in my office."

Claire looked through the half-open door, this wasn't going to be easy. She pushed the door wider hoping to see the phone and trying to be careful not to knock over any of the piles of books that littered the floor. Si assured them that they were all organised into different subject areas, but she had her doubts.

Getting to the desk, the sound was louder but she still couldn't see it. She reached across the desk, nearly knocking over the photo of his two children, and lifted the thesis he was currently reading 'Unusual Asteroid Trajectories'. No, no phone. Where on earth could it be?

Claire circled around the desk knocking leaves of the dead plant Audrey from Data Analysis had given him to brighten up his space. The sound was louder. She hoped they'd hold on or she'd never find it! His half-filled cup of cold coffee had vibration waves on the surface. She lift the cup just as the phone hidden underneath stopped ringing.

She picked it up and walked over to Si who was bending over Robin's computer screen.

"Sorry, didn't catch it in time."

"Thanks Claire, no problem." Si checked the missed calls list and hit redial.

"Professor Cartwright, here, did you call?"

"Morning Cartwright." Si recognised the voice of Chuck Greenburn.

"Yes sir, how can I help?"

"I spoke to the President yesterday, they're sending a team to investigate the asteroid impact area and assess any potential problems that may arise. I suggested you would be a good choice to head the team. Your knowledge of asteroids is internationally recognised. Are you interested?" The Administrators voice was much calmer than the last time they'd spoken.

"Well, yes sir, that would be great." Si jumped at the chance to be one of the first to see the asteroid site at first hand.

"There's a British SAS team close to the area, based in Timbuktu. They're keeping the area clear of any media and they're going to examine the region first to check whether it will be safe. Once we know, you and a few others can go and have a look."

"When do we leave?"

"You fly out today ... "

"But I thought all aircraft had been grounded today!" interrupted Si. "Aren't we going to wait until we've seen what happens when the asteroid impacts? Airspace could be filled with clouds of sand!"

"The plane they've chosen is less vulnerable to air pollution, and the President wants to have a team there first before the place is a media frenzy. We've kept everyone away so far on safety grounds, once the asteroid has impacted, I expect all hell will break loose!"

"OK sir, I see the problem. Any scientific information could be destroyed once the place is over-run with the worlds media."

"Precisely, because we're nearly seven thousand miles away, the Air-force transport will take-off today. You'll get there some time after the impact. Can you be packed and at LA Airport in three hours?"

"Yes sir, I'm sure I can. What about the equipment we'll need?" asked Si.

"Don't worry, that's all been taken care of, just get your butt over there before the plane takes off!" With that the phone clicked.

Without much time to think, he grabbed his lap-top and a few papers from his desk relating to the Asteroid and it's projected impact point and rushed out of the office. Two hours later, he was on Interstate 105 following a black and white State Patrol car that had arrived at his home to escort him through the LA traffic to the airport. They led him through the back entrance of the airport to a parking area away from the main terminals. An old Douglas C-133 transport loomed over them. Pallets and vehicles queued to be loaded.

A uniformed man approached him. "Professor Cartwright?" Si nodded, showing his ID card. "Please follow me sir."

"What about the car?"

"If you'll leave me the keys we'll get it stored while you're away."

Si grabbed his suitcase from the boot of the Jag, tossed the marine the keys and followed him to the loading ramp.

"We take-off in twenty minutes sir," stated the Marine. He pointed, "the steps are over there, have a good flight."

Si climbed the steps and passed through the doorway into a small cabin with about twenty airline type seats which were already half full.

"Can I take your case sir?" Another Marine met him as he entered. "Sit anywhere you want."

"Thanks," he settled into the nearest vacant seat. The cabin was full of tension, everyone looking around nervously as the pilot started the engines.

***

Around the world, everything had stopped. Eyes were glued to television screens or stared at the sky. In some areas of the world people watched a second sun, getting ever larger.

Stock markets wobbled again, governments struggled. Drunks wandered the streets and people started to riot. Religious organisations predicted a disaster of biblical proportions only second to the great flood. New age religions predicted man-kinds reconnection with the earth. Everything ground to a halt as people turned to televisions to watch news reports continually updating the position of the asteroid. A strange excitement infected the world.

***

In the Sahara desert, a tuareg camel train headed east. They stopped and stared at two suns glaring down. One of the suns grew slowly larger. They dismounted from their camels and knelt to face the new sun. The camels shuffled and snorted.

It was unerringly quiet as the incandescent ball of heat shot overhead trailing a plume of glittering particles.

Behind the awe inspiring sight, the sand rose in a wall sweeping towards them across the desert. As the wall hit them, the silence was shattered with the sound of a thousand express trains. The tribesmen prostrated themselves on the ground, the camels reared and bucked. But within seconds, it was silence again.

The tuareg stood up, shook the sand from their clothes and turned to watch a mushroom cloud of brilliant colour erupt on the horizon. A few seconds later the ground trembled beneath their feet as they felt the impact.

***

High above the Atlantic after a refuelling stop in the Azores, Si dozed, unable to sleep in the uncomfortable seat. No-one seemed to be able to settle, wondering what they were likely to find. They had been on the move for sixteen hours, still another seven hours to go before they reached their destination.

Earlier, the pilot had described how the C-133 had been pulled out of retirement and leased by the US Government. The Douglas had been chosen because the airstrip at Timbuktu would be too small for a C-5 Galaxy, the current air-force transport. The pilot had expressed concerns about the ability of the airstrip at Timbuktu to take even the C-133! It was designed for short landings on unprepared airstrips, but it was going to be tight.

After take-off, Si had chatted to the team he'd been given, a well thought out balance of skills. A mining engineer, a geologist, a mapping expert and a technical secretary.

As they crossed the Atlantic, the asteroid struck Africa. Far from the apocalyptic devastation that had been feared, the impact had hardly raised a murmur. Scientific institutions from around the world had all reported the same, an impact of 1.3 on the Richter scale, almost common-place.

Why so little trouble? The team developed a theory. The Magma bubble under North Africa must have absorbed the impact like a giant shock-absorber. All of the energy had dissipated into the molten rock below as well as being cushioned by the Sahara sand.

The asteroid couldn't have picked a better spot to hit the earth. The sand clouds that should have been created hadn't appeared either. They had no idea why. This was going to be a very interesting asteroid. Si couldn't wait to get there to start his investigation.

Chapter Three

Two hundred miles north of Timbuktu.

"How far now?" asked SAS Captain John Pullman as the Puma Helicopter sped low across the desert towards the crater just over eight hours after impact. They'd waited for any problems the impact might have caused to appear before starting the mission. Apart from a minor tremor in the ground and an audible rumble that reached them twenty minutes after the impact, they wouldn't have known the event that had been so feared by the world's population had happened.

"Should be able to see the site as we clear this ridge sir." The Helicopter Weapons Systems officer, Corporal Dan Johnson was huddled over his display staring at the readouts from the integrated radar and missile-approach warning system. "I haven't picked up any increased radiation levels yet." As they crested the rise, rainbow light radiated from the desert. "Oh my God! Sir ... can you see this?"

"Jesus! ... what is that?" Pullman tried to focus on the amazing sight that was unfolding before them.

The sheer beauty of the spectacle left them all speechless. The desert surface was transformed into a multi-coloured magic carpet, the colours changed and shimmered.

"That's not on the satellite maps, must be the edge of the crater," Corporal Johnson shouted, above the noise of the two Turbomeca Turmo 3-C4 turbine engines.

"Take us higher. I want to see the full extent of this," Pullman commanded. "Are you getting this on video?" he shouted to the soldier seated next to him.

"Yes, sir," confirmed the soldier, who was manipulating the Weapons Guidance Systems camera mounted under the nose of the Puma.

They crossed the 30 metre high ridge, which formed the edge of an ellipse about three kilometres long and two kilometres wide on the flat surface of the Sahara, and the true beauty hit them. An iridescent funnel, burrowing into the Sahara, changing and shimmering as their viewpoint shifted, reflecting the rays of the overhead sun. Around the crater was a band of constantly changing colour about a kilometre wide that had settled outside the ridge.

"Set us down at the edge, just outside the coloured band," ordered Pullman.

The Puma sank towards the surface and settled in a cloud of sand. Turbines spun down to idle and Pullman climbed out of the side door. Instinctively, he ducked beneath the spinning rotors and walked the short distance to the strange coloured surface. He bent down to examine the ground. Digging his hand into the desert, he held the grains up to the sun.

In his palm were tiny balls that looked like glass beads sitting on top of the hot sand. Colours of the rainbow flickered and changed as he moved his hand, the light split by hundreds of tiny prisms. He opened a small plastic bag and dropped in the grains. Putting the bag in his pocket, he returned to the Puma. "OK, we'll fly into the crater and check for any radiation problems."

The noise from the Puma's engines changed pitch as Pullman strapped himself back in to his seat. Sand swirled as the helicopter lifted above the crater.

"Keep checking for any problems," Pullman instructed. "Let me know if anything abnormal appears."

They crested the ridge and the pilot positioned the helicopter over the centre of the crater. It descended slowly. Corporal Johnson, who was constantly checking his instruments, kept his thumb raised to indicate everything was OK.

The walls of the crater were covered in the same material Pullman had examined on the surface, although it appeared smoother. About halfway down, 75 metres below the surface, Johnson shouted, "temperature is rising sir. Infra-red indicates a hot object buried below the surface in the centre of the crater. Too hot for us if we go much deeper."

"OK, hold it here. Let's scan the crater. I want to gather as much Intel as possible before we leave. Full video scan, temperatures, in fact any readings we can take. Slowly circle the sides at this height," instructed Pullman, "then, while we're refuelling, we can upload the information back to Headquarters."

The Puma slowly circled the crater as various readings were taken. Half way around the scan Johnson spotted something. "Sir, there are some shapes sticking out of the side of the crater about 10 metres below us. Not sure what they are, could be exposed rock."

"Move closer," ordered Pullman to the pilot. "Can you drop a little further?"

"Yes sir," confirmed the pilot as the Puma edged closer to the odd shapes.

Pullman stared out of the side door at the protrusions. They had a strange regular shape, not like rock the outcrops he was used to seeing during his tour of duty in the Sahara. They looked almost man-made he thought, strange so far below the surface. As far as he knew, there were no stone constructions in this area. He'd covered a lot of the desert in the two months he had been stationed outside Timbuktu at the SAS Desert Training Camp.

As he looked closer, he could see, beneath the almost glass like surface of the crater a faint shape. He took a pair of binoculars from the storage rack in the side of the cabin and focused. It looked like some sort of doorway. Stone pillars topped with a lintel and what could be a copper edged door with a black centre.

"Get some photographs." He pointed to the side of the crater. A strange feeling came over him. Maybe there was going to be more to this than he'd expected.

Chapter Four

Timbuktu

Set in the back streets of Timbuktu, what passed for a bar was hot and dry despite the illicit alcohol Pullman was drinking. However, he liked this place, he could disappear into another world, away from the discipline and order that occupied his working time. He had been here too long, he was starting to feel part of the place, this was his time to move on.

The door darkened and he looked around to see Mary enter. She'd arrived there on sabbatical a month ago to study the thousands of manuscripts scattered around this isolated town. Mary worked at the University of Sankore in Timbuktu, apparently the first University in the world.

"Hi Mary, can I get you a drink?" Pullman enjoyed her company. Although she was a Professor in Pre-human Archaeology and Ancient Texts at Durham University, she had a very open down-to-earth manner that he liked.

She was on the rebound from a romance and Timbuktu had been a convenient excuse to leave her life in England. Apparently, they'd been very close until he'd decided that her best friend was more fun. She was happy that Timbuktu would put enough space between them for her to start to look forward again.

She had needed some comfort and Pullman was happy to oblige. It hadn't lasted long, but they still managed to remain good friends. He didn't want a relationship, he moved around too much, and she hadn't really had time to got over her boyfriend.

"Thought I'd find you in here ... any info on the asteroid impact?" Mary liked Pullman. For all his brash exterior, she knew underneath he was an intelligent, sensitive man. He'd never married, he was married to the SAS, but he was good company.

"We went out to the crater site today. It was unbelievable! I've got some photo's here on my camera ... take a look." Pullman flicked to the first picture of the crater and passed the camera to Mary. He knew he could trust her to be discreet and images of the site would soon be global news anyway.

Mary scrolled through the images, her eyes getting wider, emitting small gasps as each image was displayed. "This is amazing! It's so beautiful. Who would have thought something like this could be created by such a threatening object."

Pullman nodded, remembering the sheer beauty he'd seen.

"Hold on, what's this?" Mary turned the camera so Pullman could see the image. Mary had reached the pictures of the doorway.

"I've no idea. You can just make it out behind the glassy surface. Have you any thoughts?" Pullman asked.

"None, but I'd love to get a closer look. Are you going back again?" The excitement in Mary's voice was noticeable.

"I sent the information we collected back to HQ on a secure transmission, but I've had no new orders. We're waiting for some specialists to arrive. A joint US/UK team are on their way.

Should arrive early tomorrow. My instructions are to provide any support and security I can."

"I'd love to get on the team. Who's in charge?" asked Mary.

"I think it's a Professor from LA, Simon Cartwright," he responded.

"What ... Cartwright. Well, well, Si Cartwright, I met him at a symposium in London a few years ago. Clever man, specialises in asteroids and such. Maybe there ***is*** a chance I can jump aboard." Mary thought back to their last meeting. Si had been interested in some work she had done with pre-historic tools made from meteor fragments. They'd got on well.

"When do they arrive?" Mary asked.

"About 18:00 hours, you'll know when they get here, they're coming in a C-133 probably shake up the whole town," smiled Pullman.

Mary continued to look through the photo's, zooming in to examine small details, especially around the doorway. "You can almost see what looks like symbols above the door. Not clear enough to identify them, but they don't look random."

Pullman remembered the sample he had taken at the site and pulled the bag out of his pocket. He passed it to Mary who turned it over in her hand. She held the bag up to the light from the door. "Looks like glass beads," she said. "Sand is basically powdered glass, so I'm guessing the heat from the impact has melted the sand."

As they were talking, a Tuareg tribesman entered the bar wearing the traditional blue Tagelmust which covered most of his face, and as Mary held the bag to the light, he approached. "I wish not to offend, but may I see?" Mary looked at

Pullman, who shrugged, so she held the bag up to the stranger. "Such beauty, how our view can change when we see things in different lights."

He looked directly into Mary's eyes with a dark almost trance-like stare. Mary thought his eyes shone for a moment but the image was gone before she could focus. "You must examine this further, it is your destiny." The stranger turned and was gone as quickly as he'd appeared.

A strange silence and calmness had fallen over the bar. The locals had all turned to look at Mary with compassionate faces. A few touched their foreheads before turning back to their conversations. The bar came back to life.

"Wow ... what was that about?" Pullman exclaimed.

"Did you feel his presence?" asked Mary. "Such a calmness, and his eyes ... I shall never forget his eyes."

"Looks like you've got to get on that expedition," joked Pullman. "You've had your orders."

Chapter Five

Timbuktu airstrip

Mary was waiting at the airstrip just outside Timbuktu, watching the beautiful orange of the Saharan sunset, when she heard the sound of the C-133 approaching from the east over the road to Timbuktu.

As the noise increased she spotted the large silver transport. It flashed over-head with a deafening noise from its four Pratt & Whitney turboprops.

The pilot was checking the small airstrip as he banked the massive plane to circle round for his final approach. He lined up for the runway and sank onto the narrow tarmac strip.

As soon as the wheels touched, the engine noise increased to a deafening roar; the pilot engaged reverse thrust to slow the heavy aircraft as rapidly as possible. Clouds of sand erupted in front of the plane and the aircraft became almost invisible as it came to a standstill a few yards from the end of the tarmac strip. Two engines roared as the massive aircraft turned around and proceeded slowly back towards the airport buildings and Mary.

Pullman strolled out of the main building. "Told you you'd know when they arrived. Bloody noisy things." Pullman was dressed in his desert camouflage, a scar on his leg clearly visible below his shorts. A shot from a sniper in Kyrgyzstan while dragging a civilian out of the line of fire, the reason for the Military Cross ribbon on his uniform.

Mary wore her long blonde hair down, cascading over her shoulders. Her hair kept the fierce desert sun off the back of her neck. She would normally wear it tied up to stop it getting in her way when reading the manuscripts, but then she was usually under cover.

She wore a short sleeved white shirt and short khaki shorts, her slender arms uncovered. Even her desert boots looked attractive at the end of her long slim legs, tanned by the African sun.

They both waited as a tall, lean man stepped from the loading ramp at the back of the plane. Si was wearing his favourite jeans, perhaps a little too faded now, with a blue denim shirt. His dark brown hair, forever uncontrolled, dropped across his blue eyes. As Si walked towards Mary and he dragged his well travelled suitcase behind him.

He extended his free hand, "Hi, I'm Simon Cartwright, you must be Captain Pullman ... hello Mary, that's a surprise ... it has been a long time."

"Yes sir, I'm Pullman, I run an SAS training operation here. I've been instructed to provide you with anything you need and to transport you to the crater."

Si nodded, "I could do with a bath and a rest. I'm exhausted, we've been on the go for the last twenty four hours."

"I've booked you into the Hotel Relais Azalai, there are a few from the media there, but there's plenty of room if anyone else in your party needs accommodation," Pullman replied.

"I'll give you a lift," offered Mary, not completely altruistically, "we can catch up on the way."

"My team will help unloading. I'll check the equipment itinerary as well. Maybe see you later." Pullman headed off towards the plane.

After Si had cleared what was euphemistically called Customs, Mary swung her battered Land Rover onto the metalled road that ran into town.

"So, what brings you to Timbuktu?" he asked.

Mary explained about the manuscripts she was researching and gave a brief description of the long history of Timbuktu.

Si enjoyed listening to an English accent again, "are you staying at the Hotel?"

"No, I rent close to the University. I like the peace and quiet of my own space. Although you wouldn't believe it, at times this is a pretty busy place."

Outside the old sports stadium, a battered sign welcomed them to 'Timbuktu, City of Three Hundred and Thirty-Three Saints'. At the edge of the city the tarmac ended and turned to sand as they swung around a roundabout with an odd shaped concrete monument at it's centre, heading for the Hotel.

Mary brought the Land Rover to a dusty stop outside the Hotel. Si grabbed his suitcase from the back and followed Mary past a line of Tuareg. Lean, olive-skinned faces swathed in black and indigo headdresses.

"Would you like to meet up later, after you've freshened up? I'm sure Pullman will be around as well," asked Mary.

Si signed in as the Receptionist found his room key. "OK, fine, give me a couple of hours." He was enjoying Mary's interest.

"I'll pick you up later," she beamed. Then she turned and left. Si watched her slim figure cross Reception and pass into the busy street.

***

Showered, changed and freshened, Si stood on the steps of the Hotel waiting for Mary. He'd managed to fend off a couple of media people, telling them he was visiting an old friend. He didn't think they believed him, but luckily they didn't recognise his name. His research wasn't exciting enough to throw him into the media limelight.

As he stared out across Timbuktu, dusk settled, donkeys struggled down the street with impossibly high bales of hay as tall figures in dark robes goaded them on. An odd battered vehicle picked its way through sandy streets. He caught sight of Mary, her blonde hair being sucked out of the side window of the Land Rover. One working headlight flashing and dipping. She skidded to a halt in a cloud of sand and waved him in.

"There's a sort of bar we use. Nothing special, but peaceful, away from all the media. Is that OK?" asked Mary.

"Sure ... you're the Tour Guide around here." Si smiled.

Mary parked the Land Rover next to the bar. Pullman was already inside at the usual table.

"Hi, Si, what can I get you? Usual for you Mary?" Pullman signalled the bar owner. Mary nodded.

"Thanks, I'll have a beer, it seems to get pretty hot here. Need something to cool down." Si was already showing signs of discomfort in the heat.

"Believe me, it gets hotter ... how do you want to play this?" Pullman asked.

"Well, I'll be led by you." Si conceded. "You know the area far better than I do. I'd like to get to the site as soon as possible."

"I've got some pictures here on my camera. Take a look," said Pullman.

After scrolling through the images, Si was even more confused.

"This is from the edge of crater," Pullman pulled out the plastic bag with the sample he had collected. "Have you seen anything like this before?"

Si held the bag to the light and then emptied the grains into his palm. "This is unusual. Normally, you'd expect to find Tektite material like this around a meteorite impact, but it's usually dark green. There is some light green glass like material around a site in the Czech republic, but this is almost clear. Perhaps, because it impacted into sand, there aren't any mineral impurities to provide a definite colour. This site is going to cause a few of our theories to be reviewed. When do we start?"

"I suggest we start early tomorrow. I'll get the helicopters loaded with enough equipment to set up camp and to have a preliminary look at the crater. How many of you will be travelling out to the site?" Pullman asked.

"There's about six specialists, plus the Marines that came with us. You'll have to check with their commander to see if they want to come and how many. I suspect he'll want to leave a contingent here to look after the rest of the equipment," suggested Si.

"OK, leave it to me. We'll meet at the airstrip at 06:00 hours before it gets too hot. It's a couple of hours to the crater. Should set up camp well before mid-day ... Cheers." Pullman raised the bottle of Budweiser and took a long swig.

"Did you take a look at the pictures of the object just below the surface?" Mary asked.

"Certainly did, not sure what that's about. Will it be very easy to get down the side of the crater?" Si asked Pullman.

"I'll bring along some structural equipment. Should be able to rig some sort of platform, be enough to give you safe access should the side of the crater start to slip."

"I think it's something man-made," Mary didn't want to drop the subject. "There appears to be some sort of symbols cut into the stone. As the resident archaeologist, I'd love to come along and help in any way I can."

"Why not ... is it OK with you?" Si looked at Pullman.

"Sure, Mary knows this place fairly well, I don't think she'll be a problem." Pullman smiled, pleased she was going to share in the adventure.

"OK, let's have another beer," said Si. "This one's on me," as he waved at the bar owner to bring another round.

Chapter Six

The Crater

It was first light, everyone was milling around the three Puma helicopters as the last cases of equipment were being strapped down. Mary and Si stood patiently to one side with the other specialists and watched Pullman issue the last instructions to his men. A few Marines were helping, although most, as Si had guessed, were staying behind.

All of the personnel were to travel in the lead helicopter with Pullman, the other two Pumas were to transport the equipment needed to set-up the base camp.

Pullman waved them over and everyone climbed aboard. The civilians strapped themselves into lightweight chairs and the military personnel stood holding onto support straps. Pullman gave the command and the helicopter engines spun into life, they lifted from the tarmac and headed north towards the crater.

The two hour journey passed quickly as Si and Mary took turns to speculate on the strange images, examining them in detail using Pullman's camera. Corporal Johnson shouted to Pullman when they were nearing the crater and told them to look out of the front windscreen.

The sight that opened up was just as impressive as it had been the first time. The early morning sun created amazing patterns as it mixed with shadows from the surrounding dunes. Si and Mary were dumbstruck. The photo's hadn't done it justice. The sheer scale of the spectacle and the myriad of shimmering colours took their breath away.

"Drop her down on the eastern edge just outside the crater," Pullman instructed. He turned to Mary and Si, "it'll take us a couple of hours to set up camp. I suggest you stay inside the helicopter to avoid the sun until we can offer some sort of protection."

They both nodded as the helicopter settled in the sand. Pullman's men and the few Marines jumped out and made for the other two helicopters as they landed in a line. Side doors were pulled open and pallets manhandled out of the Pumas.

To distract himself, Si opened his laptop and examined the data from the asteroid impact. He then transferred the images from Pullman's camera via it's data card reader.

He turned to Mary, "I think the reason why there was no major earth tremor was because we're sitting on top of a massive magma cap. I'm guessing it absorbed the impact energy rather than reflecting it back to the surface. Looking at the ground around the crater, I think the conversion of the sand to glass is the reason why there wasn't a massive sand cloud. The glass pellets were too heavy to get blown into the wind and they settled around the crater ... so tell me, how long do you plan to be in Africa?"

The question caught Mary by surprise. Oddly enough, she hadn't really thought that far ahead. "I'm not sure. Perhaps another five or six months ... let's have another look at those photo's on your laptop. The bigger images might show more detail."

Si clicked open the folder and turned the laptop so they could both examine the screen. Mary leaned closer to him to get a clearer look and felt a warmth that was nothing to do with the African sun. Her hair brushed his bare forearm as he clicked through the images.

"Hold it on that one. Can you zoom in? Have you got any image enhancing software?" Mary was desperate to try and understand the vague shapes above what she was convinced was a doorway.

"I have ... we use it to enhance images from Hubble. Hold on I'll run the picture through." He expertly flicked around the mouse pad and keyboard as the software was loaded. "Let's see what happens."

The grainy detail of the enlarged image slowly sharpened. The shapes above the doorway materialised. At the left hand end of the lintel was a circle with eight short lines radiating out, at the right hand end there was a rectangle within a rectangle short side to the bottom. In between the two symbols was an elongated triangle on its side with the sharp end touching the centre of the inner rectangle and the wide end near the circle.

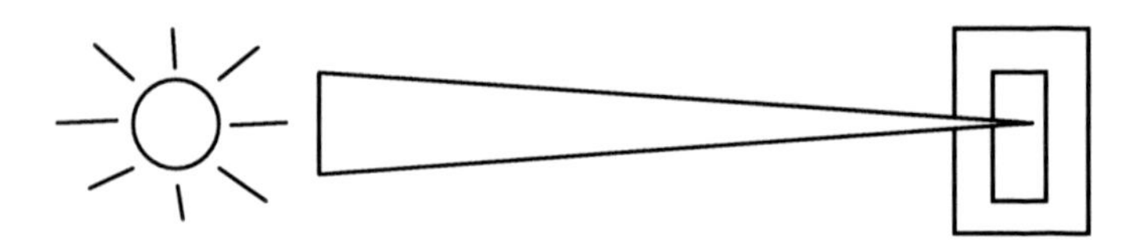

"Have you seen anything like this before?" He asked Mary.

"No, nothing," I'm stunned, "it's very simplistic considering the skill that's gone into constructing the doorway. I'm not sure what to make of it. It appears to show the sun focusing it's rays on the centre of the door, but that seems too simple an explanation. Maybe we'll be able to tell more close-up."

While they'd been in deep discussion, the camp had been erected. A large desert camouflage canopy gave shade to a number of small tents. There was a long table with benches either side and two large tents at each end.

Pullman, followed by Corporal Johnson, walked over to the helicopter and leaned in the door. "Your accommodation is ready. We'll have power in about ten minutes. Just got to fire up the generator. We've put it behind that sand dune so the noise won't disturb us in the night."

Turning to Corporal Johnson he said, "Johnson, monitor the Radar and let me know if you see anything strange, oh, and check the radiation readings just to make sure nothing's changed since we were last here."

"Yes sir," Corporal Johnson climbed into the helicopter and took his seat at the Weapons Radar console. "Everything appears to be the same, sir."

Mary and Si grabbed their cases and made their way towards the camp.

"You've each got one of those small tents." Pullman pointed under the canopy. "A bit cramped I'm afraid but the canopy should keep off the worst of the sun. I'll take you up to the edge of the crater when you've dumped your cases and you can have a look."

Mary and Si picked two tents next to each other, unzipped the fronts and pushed in their cases. The tents were already equipped with a tropical sleeping bag, a bottle of water and some eating utensils.

Pullman led the way to the top of the ridge. The surface crunched under their feet as they trod on the millions of tiny glass balls. Rainbow colours swirled around them. The last part of the climb was a bit of a struggle as the sand slipped away under their feet. Si took Mary's hand as they reached the top to give her some extra support. As they crested the ridge, an amazing scene opened out before them.

"Don't go too close to the edge, I'm not sure how safe the ground is yet. Wouldn't want you visiting the asteroid before it was time," Pullman smiled.

The three of them stood back from the edge and gazed in wonder. The conical shape of the crater looked like it was lined in glass. The sun reflected off the surface in a dazzling display of colours.

Si realised he was still holding Mary's hand. It felt oddly comfortable and she didn't resist. He spotted the place further down the side where the doorway was just visible. "It's there, do you think you can get us access to that? Looks pretty precarious to me!"

Pullman liked a challenge, "I think so, we can hang some cables down the crater and lower a platform. You might have to climb down on a rope, but we can make sure it's safe. Are either of you scared of heights?"

"I'll try not to look down," said Mary, "nothing's going to put me off getting a look at that!"

"I've done a bit of climbing in my younger days, I'm sure I'll be OK." Si sounded more confident than he felt. Rock climbing when a teenager as part of his Duke of Edinburgh Award was a long time ago.

"Good, I'll get the men organised. Might as well start as soon as we can." Pullman turned and started back down the slope, "I'll give you a shout when we're ready."

Mary and Si lingered a little longer, entranced by the rainbow colours as they danced around the crater to the movement of the sun across the sky. They finally returned to camp to wait for Pullman's call.

Soldiers hurried around, collected equipment from the helicopters and carried it to the edge of the crater. A structure slowly took shape above the exposed doorway. After a couple of hours, Pullman returned to camp and found Mary and Si sitting at the long table under the canopy chatting and drinking tea brewed by the SAS cook.

"We're just about ready. I've had a couple of men go down and check everything. Seems pretty safe, so now it's up to you two."

Mary and Si jumped to their feet, eager to check out the strange opening. "Lead the way," said Si. "We can't wait."

Chapter Seven

The Library

It took Pullman, Si and Mary, ten minutes to get to the impressive structure now assembled on the edge. Cables, anchored to some heavy equipment, travelled over the top of the structure and down into the crater. The two scientists peered over the edge to see a platform about two metres square resting against the side.

"We've positioned the platform at the base of the structure and there's a ladder on the platform if you need to get a look at the top of the doorway. There was a coating of fused glass beads over the door but my men have cleared them away. It all seems pretty solid, so come on, let's strap you into the safety harnesses." Even Pullman found it difficult to hide his excitement.

Si volunteered to go first and stepped backwards over the edge, he part abseiled, part walked down to the platform while Pullman's men let out the safety rope.

As Mary was lowered down, she kept looking up; looking down didn't seem like a good idea. Finally her feet touched the edge of the platform. She stopped for a moment to regain her composure and looked at the structure in front of her. She had seen nothing like it, either first hand, or in documents from the many archaeological digs she'd examined.

The base of the door was a flat polished stone step about two metres wide. Standing on either end were two square pillars three metres tall. Carved in relief into the pillars were various animal figures in intricate detail, reminiscent of the pillars she'd seen in Golbleki Tepi. These were topped with the lintel she'd found so intriguing. Framed in the doorway was what appeared to be a door. The edges were polished copper covered in a transparent film while the bulk of the centre was matt black.

There was no obvious opening or mechanism on the door, it was completely smooth and recessed into the frame. Si tried to push the door but it was fixed solidly in place. "I don't think there's much doubt that it's meant to be a door, but how do we open it and what on earth is on the other side?"

"Let's take another look at those symbols," suggested Mary. "Maybe we'll deduce something."

Si grabbed the ladder on the edge of the platform and leaned it against the left hand pillar. "You'd better take a look, it might make more sense to you. I'll hold the ladder."

"Thanks ... here goes," said Mary. As she climbed a few rungs the platform moved slightly as the point of balance shifted. Her knuckles went white as she gripped the ladder. "Did I tell you I don't like heights!"

She braced herself and studied the symbols. "It looks just the same as the enhanced images we looked at on your computer."

She climbed back down. "Do you think it's some sort of key? I'm wondering if it's telling us to focus the sun's rays onto the door?"

"That would make sense, although I can't imagine how it would open the door. Let's get back and see if Pullman can sort something out."

At the top they discussed Mary's idea with Pullman. He said he thought there might be a way and wandered off to talk to some of his men. A couple of soldiers went back in the direction of the camp. "Don't know if my idea will work or if it will give enough light, but I can't think of anything else we can do with what we have here."

The two men returned about twenty minutes later with a satellite communication dish and an aluminium foil blanket.

Si guessed Pullman's plan. "Brilliant idea, it might just work."

The men covered the dish with the blanket creating a crude parabolic mirror. Held at the right angle to the overhead sun, it produced a powerful beam that quickly set a scrap piece of cardboard alight.

"OK, let's get it down to the platform ... careful how you position it, I don't want anyone incinerated," shouted Pullman to the two men preparing to take the dish down to the platform.

After the soldiers returned, Mary and Si descended to the platform. Si lifted the dish and angled it so the suns rays focused onto the centre of the black panel and waited. They felt heat radiating from the door. Si was finding it difficult to hold the dish steady when suddenly, there was a clunk and the door slowly gaped open.

"Must've expanded and released some sort of lock." Si put the dish down. "Wait a minute for the door to cool ... can you see anything inside?"

Mary couldn't wait and peered into the mysterious black space, "shine the dish in to give some light."

He picked up the dish and carefully aimed the sunlight through the doorway. The darkness exploded into light. The beam had hit a crystalline structure on the floor of a room and light was being radiated in every direction.

As she looked in her mouth dropped. An enormous room was being lit by the crystal. "Wow, this is amazing ... it's some sort of building. I can just about see walls and tiered steps ... we need to get some light in here ... pass me the torch and put down the dish, I don't want you to fry me!"

Si carefully put the dish down and passed Mary a torch. She disappeared through the doorway and stepped into a large room about thirty to forty metres wide and much longer. The walls she could see were constructed from large interlocking bricks, she couldn't properly make out the end wall as the torch beam wasn't strong enough. The air was cool, quite a contrast to the heat outside. Above all, there was on overwhelming sense of peace

Si spoke into the radio. "Pullman, are you there? We've opened the door. Inside is an enormous room, we're just entering now to check it out."

"Be careful," came the reply, "we don't know how old or safe the structure is, we don't want any accidents."

"Roger that!" Si stepped through the doorway. "Oh my God! What is this place? Shine the torch at the crystal, let's see what happens."

Mary aimed the torch beam at the crystal and as it struck, the room lit up again. The crystal amplifed the meagre light provided by the torch and redirected it throughout the room. She placed the torch down against the crystal and moved in further.

Against each side wall, for the length of the wall, were a dozen stone tiers about one metre high and one and half metres wide. Against the back of these steps were long rows of boxes made from copper.

"I wonder what these contain? Perhaps it's some sort of burial chamber, could be ashes or bones inside," Mary speculated.

"They look too small to contain bones, you'd have to chop up the bodies to fit them in. Not very respectful. Let's take a look." Si examined the box. "There's a lid, can't shift it, seems to be sealed with something." He pulled out his Swiss Army knife and tried to push the blade into the join.

Scraps of the sealant cracked off. Mary picked some up, rubbed it between her fingers and smelt. "It could be beeswax but there haven't been bees here for tens of thousands of years."

Si scrapped the blade around the join and thrust the blade into a small gap. As he levering the lid there was a sharp crack as the blade broke, Si cursed as he scuffed his knuckles on the side of the box. Ignoring the blood, he forced the broken blade back into the gap. This time, the lid cracked open, a sweet smell filled their nostrils. Mary reached inside and pulled out a sheet of translucent material.

"This is incredible!" She couldn't believe her eyes. The sheet had writing she'd never seen before. The uniformity of the script was surprising. Neat rows of symbols or letters, above which was a simple drawing of a square.

"Is this anything like the manuscripts you're studying in Timbuktu?" Si had joined her on the step and was staring at the sheet in her hand.

"No, I've seen just about every recorded language, and there's nothing like this." Mary was dumbfounded.

She moved down the row and examined a few more boxes. "They all contain dozens of these sheets and seem to get more complex as I move along the row. Perhaps this is some sort of store room for knowledge, a Library perhaps?"

"If all the boxes are like this one, there must be hundreds, perhaps thousands of these sheets!" Si exclaimed. "I'm not sure if they'll survive the hot sun though. Have you noticed how cool it is in here. Must've been at a stable temperature since it was buried. There are no windows either, that's why no sand has got in to fill the room. It's probably airtight."

"We'll take some pictures, I can use your laptop to transmit a few to some colleagues in Durham, see if they have any ideas." Mary was already making a mental list of people to contact.

She held the first half dozen sheets while Si photographed them. She then carefully replaced them in their boxes and closed the lids.

"Right, let's see if we can find out what we've found." Mary led the way back out onto the platform. "Can we pull the door too to stop any sunlight or moisture entering the room? The desert air can get quite damp at night."

Si pulled the heavy door until it was open just a crack. They contacted Pullman and started the ascent to the top of the ridge.

Back in camp, Mary emailed the pictures to a small selection of colleagues and Si emailed his boss to tell him what they'd found.

High above the earth, in a geostationary orbit, a communications satellite picked up the transmissions and forwarded them to England and America. A second private satellite in a similar orbit also picked up the transmissions and directed them to a third destination.

Chapter Eight

A surprise visit

"Sir," Corporal Johnson's voice crackled in Pullman's ear piece. "We've got incoming ... very fast. I'd say it was an F-15."

"What the ... " a shadow flashed over head, followed by the loud roar of a fast jet travelling at 600 miles an hour. "Everybody, get under cover," Pullman shouted.

***

The F-15 pilot rolled the plane out of it's climb and commenced a run back towards the crater. "Target identified, there appears to be some work going on down the side of the crater. Instructions? ... OK, understood. Collapse the side of the crater and then close down the site. I'm activating weapons systems now, out."

***

Pullman watched the matt-black F-15 pull into a vertical climb over the crater, rotate and sweep down.

"He's coming in for another run, are the weapons systems on-line?" shouted Pullman.

"Yes sir, everything's operational," confirmed Johnson.

It was fortunate he'd had the foresight to leave Johnson at his console in the Puma monitoring the Weapon Systems Radar. He always took notice of his intuition, it had saved him and his men many times in the past. Even luckier, the Puma was facing in the direction of the now rapidly approaching jet.

***

The F15's Weapons Operator shouted to the pilot. "Can't use heat sensing, deserts to warm. Laser targeting is going haywire with all the reflections from whatever's covering the surface. I'll have to use visual aiming, tricky at this speed, still, here goes."

***

"Their targeting systems are active. Here it comes!" Johnson spoke just as a missile detached itself from the F-15 and hurtled towards them. Within seconds, the missile shot overhead, it just missed the top of the far side of the crater and exploded a few hundred metres away in a cloud of sand.

The jet followed, climbed again and rotated for another run.

"They're trying to hit the inside of the crater! Johnson, bring that plane down! Use the Stingers, both of them. Don't lock missiles until the last minute, we can't afford to give them time to use avoidance tactics. Is that clear?" Pullman realised that if the F-15 decided to target the helicopters, they would be sitting ducks.

"Yes sir." Johnson watched the F-15 approach, this time from a higher altitude, giving him more time to target the plane.

Fortunately, the Puma had been fitted with a pair of next generation AIM-92 Stinger air-to-air missiles which were being evaluated in desert conditions. Pullman hoped they'd work as they would normally be fired from a helicopter in flight. He wasn't sure about a ground launch. Anyway, there was no time to get the helicopter into the air, and if they did, it would be no match for the F-15.

Whoosh, whoosh, the two Stingers leapt from the missile rack and streaked towards the jet. With a closing speed near a thousand miles per hour, one missile shot into the air intake of the F-15 within seconds while the other missed by a few yards.

The plane exploded in an incandescent fire-ball. The crew didn't have time to eject. Red hot metal fragments showered down as the larger pieces shot overhead with enough momentum to clear the crater and hit the desert on the other side.

Silence returned as Pullman walked over to the Puma.

"Well done Johnson. Wasn't sure that was going to work ... what was that all about? ... Is everyone OK?" He shouted into his throat mic.

His team confirmed no casualties.

The Captain of the Marines jogged over, "what the hell's going on?"

"I wish I knew. The plane didn't have any markings. Could have come from anywhere. There are dozens of F-15's scattered across the globe, owned by some pretty shaky governments. I've even heard there's a free-lance one out there somewhere," Pullman pondered.

"Well, there's one less now!" The marine Captain said wryly.

"I'd like to think that's the end of it, but I have a bad feeling." Pullman was trying to piece together what had happened and what he would be doing if he was on the other side. "Just blowing us up doesn't make any sense. Perhaps they're trying to eliminate what we've found? But my unit would send a team to find out what had happened and if we were strewn all over the desert, questions would be asked. I have a feeling a second force is on it's way to carry out a clean-up operation.

"Johnson, find the pilot. I want this helicopter air-borne in five minutes and I want a wide electronics sweep of the area completed in ten. Oh, and load two more Stingers."

"Yes sir," Johnson sprinted towards the tents.

Three minutes later the puma lifted above the camp. After a full scan Johnson reported, "nothing on the radar at the moment sir."

"OK, put the Puma on top of that outcrop to the east and keep a constant radar watch. Let me know if you spot anything strange." Pullman wasn't going to take any chances.

He gathered the rather anxious civilians together and told them of his concerns about the possibility of a further visit and asked them to keep close to the camp.

Chapter Nine

Return to the library

The following morning around 6am, Si and Mary were hurriedly descending to the platform in the crater. Equipped with portable lanterns, they intended to make a more thorough search of the Library. Pullman had warned they might have to leave the site quickly if his worst fears were confirmed, so they intended to try and gather as much information as possible in this visit.

Mary set about examining more of the strange documents. She started to see a pattern emerge. The tablets on the bottom steps all followed a similar theme. A symbol or image with text beneath. Mary considered the possibility that whoever had written the tablets was trying to provide a means of decoding the language. She wondered if the symbol was described in simple terms in the text allowing a vocabulary to be built up enabling the more complex texts to be read.

She moved higher up the shelves to find the tablets did get more complex. Some with complex diagrams, and some with no symbols at all. She rushed back to the bottom step and started to compare tablets looking for similar text patterns. Then, by comparing the symbols, she started to deduce the meanings of certain strings, maybe 'straight' was used on the tablets with squares, rectangles and triangles for instance. maybe 'angle' also appeared.

One tablet had what could only be numbers, one bar with a word underneath, two bars, a different word, three bars yet another, dots were added all the way across and down the tablet reminiscent of the Mayan number system. She started noting down the various words and her translation. The word for four, appeared on the square symbol tablet, the word for three on the triangle. It was a painstaking process as she was slowly built the vocabulary of a lost civilisation.

Si explored further back into the library and found another doorway. This was similar to the copper entrance door, but it had a horizontal lever half way down. Si tried to move the lever, pulling, pushing, lifting and after some effort managed to push it down. The door swung open and in the dim light, he could just make out another room. He looked back to check Mary was still engrossed in the tablets and then entered.

His flash-light illuminated a large circular room with a crystal suspended in the centre of the ceiling. There were eight long stone troughs on the floor radiating out like petals from the crystal. Si walked over to the closest and jumped back in surprise. Staring back at him was the remains of a creature, human like, but not quite human. He estimated the body to be about eight feet tall very slim with long arms and legs. The head was tapered down to the chin and was much bigger than a human head. He checked the other troughs and found their contents were all similar.

Entering the troughs was an extension of the crystal which touched the top of the skull of each skeleton. He called Mary, his voice echoed around the chamber. When she arrived, he pointed the flash-light into the trough.

"Good God! What on earth are these?" She recovered her composure and started to study the first body. She carefully lifted some fragments of cloth to examine the decomposed remains. Moving to the head, she took out a small ruler from her shorts and measured the skull.

"Do you realise, the brain cavity is fifty percent bigger than ours?" She'd examined remains from burials all around the world, but she hadn't seen anything like this.

"Are they aliens?" Si asked, completely at a loss.

"I don't think so, ... there are definite similarities to humans, but also significant differences. It's almost as if they are our long lost cousins. A bit like Neanderthals, only these seem much more developed. I've got no idea how old. It's a pity there isn't any equipment in Timbuktu to try and date them."

Si flashed the torch around the circular walls. The stones were cut into smaller and smaller blocks as the room tapered into a self supporting dome. The intricately carved crystal, shaped a bit like an octopus, hung from the centre as if it had dropped through the centre. All around it were carved the same symbols they had seen on the tablets. The crystal had a milky consistency that seemed to pulse in their torch light.

"Have you seen anything like this chamber before?" he asked.

"Not really. It's not like the burial tombs in the Pyramids, they're all rectangular and quite plain. Nor is it like the Mayan temples. No, I haven't seen anything similar. This place is certainly full of surprises. If we could decipher those tablets, I'm certain we would get a lot of answers. Perhaps we'd then be able to translate the symbols on the crystal."

Chapter Ten

Somewhere in the Sahara

Three black Apache helicopters and a large black Chinook swept low across the desert, having refuelled at a desolate spot in Egypt. Meir Shavit, an officer in the Collections Department of Mossad, the Israel Intelligence Service, was in the Chinook. He'd carried out special assignments for Mossad for the last fifteen years, after leaving the Israel army. However, this assignment was very different. His instructions had been very clear, 'sterilise the site and leave no trace.'

He'd been approached ten years ago to provide 'tactical' support to an organisation of whom he had no knowledge, which was unusual considering his current employment should have made him aware of any clandestine organisations.

The radio operator turned to him, "we've lost contact sir. Total radio failure. We've also lost any radar contact. The F-15 appeared twice above the radar horizon, but hasn't been identified since. Seems we have a plane down, sir."

"I wonder if they completed the mission before they disappeared?" Shavit became uneasy. "We might have more to clean up than we thought. Keep looking for any contact and let me know if you find anything."

"Just had another radar contact sir, slow moving, I'd guess it was a helicopter. It's dropped below the radar again," shouted the radio operator.

"Seems they might be on to us, keep communication channels open and report the loss of the F-15 back to base."

Shavit didn't want this mission. Something had told him to keep away, but orders were orders and he wasn't given any option. How could they fill a hole in the ground? This wasn't the sort of work he was used to, he hadn't been in charge of a construction team before.

"Send one of the Apaches on ahead. Let's find out what we're getting into."

"Yes sir," the radio operator issued the order to the lead Apache. It accelerated away from the lumbering Chinook which was loaded with heavy earth-moving equipment.

***

Pullman received the news he was dreading.

"Four targets heading this way, should arrive in a couple hours sir," Corporal Johnson confirmed.

"OK, return to base. Looks like we're going to have company and I don't think it's going to be friendly."

Pullman tried his radio to contact Si and Mary, but without success. "We haven't got time to send someone to get them out of the Library. They're probably safer there than up here! First, we need to move the remaining civilians out of the area." He turned to the pilot. "I want you to take the civilians twenty miles to the south. We passed over a rock outcrop on the way here which I know has some caves, they should be safe enough in there. Give them a mobile radio pack and take one of the Marines with you. Oh, and keep low I don't want any radar signature. Then get back here as fast as you can."

"Yes sir."

Pullman left the Puma and headed for the camp. Fortunately, all the remaining civilians were grouped together studying the photo's of the tablets. "We've got trouble approaching. I want you all to get into that helicopter. We're going to ferry you to a safe spot. Someone will come with you and if we don't come back to pick you up, then wait twelve hours before sending a distress signal back to base at Timbuktu."

"Is it that bad?" asked the Mining Engineer. "What about Mary and Si? They're still in the Library!" Pullman's look was enough. They all got to their feet, grabbed a few belongings from their tents and headed for the Puma which was idling, waiting to go.

Pullman needed every minute to put his plan in place. "OK, gather round." There was silence as his men listened intently.

***

The lead Apache approached the area keeping low to avoid detection. The pilot swept over the crater and spotted the wreckage. He reported back that the F-15 had been destroyed and the area around the crater appeared clear. All he could see was a structure hanging down one side of the crater and an abandoned camp. It seemed the UK/US team had left in a hurry.

Shavit listened. It didn't seem logical they'd left the area. It also meant that, if they had, they may have taken some material with them which would need to be destroyed. At least that would be more like the operations he was used to. "Check the area again. Scan a couple of kilometres around the crater. Then secure the area."

In thirty minutes, they would arrive at the crater to start the clearance work. Looked like they would be burying the remains of an F-15 as well.

***

From the top of an escapement three miles from the crater, Pullman watched patiently. He saw the lead Apache arrive and scan the area. Thirty minutes later the main force, another two Apaches and a Chinook. He prayed his plan would succeed as Mary and Si were still in the Library, unaware of the activity above ground.

Timing was going to be critical and he wished he'd brought more offensive weapons. He wasn't aware someone was planning to start a war. He hoped the men descending from the helicopters were too focused on their own mission to realise what he had in mind, until it was too late.

He waited until the rotors of their helicopters had stopped. He wanted to generate as much panic as he could to give himself the psychological edge. "OK, Red One lift-off."

The sound of the Puma's engines and the throb of the rotor could be heard in the distance as the helicopter rose from behind a sand dune a few kilometres away.

***

Half a dozen men had leapt from the Chinook and made for the edge of the crater where the structure was supporting the platform. They placed explosives around the base and retreated to a safe distance before detonating the charges. The side of the crater collapsed, the structure and platform fell to the bottom. The sand started to slide down the tapered cone. As it flowed over the doorway, the entrance to the Library was engulfed.

"Sir, we have an unidentified echo on the radar," the radio operator of the Chinook called to Shavit. "Due north, about five kilometers."

"So, they've been hiding. I wondered how they managed to escape so quickly. Send an Apache to intercept and destroy," Shavit ordered.

One of the Apaches fired its engines and climbed into the sky heading North.

***

Pullman watched in despair as the crater collapsed, imprisoning Si and Mary inside. "OK, are you ready Red One?"

"Yes sir, everything's in place," replied the pilot. The Puma hung in the air just above the sand dune. "I've got him on radar. He's activating his weapon systems."

"Hold steady," ordered Pullman. The Apache drew closer, heading straight for the Puma. In a straight fight, the Puma was no match for the much smaller, better armed and more nimble Apache. But this wasn't going to be a straight fight.

As the Apache crossed a dry river bed within one kilometre of the Puma, a tell tale smoke trail left a gully below and within seconds, the hand held ground-to-air missile struck the Apache. The pilot had no time to react and the Apache crashed into a dune and exploded.

"Get to grid position two, now," ordered Pullman. The odds were starting to swing in his favour, but he had now lost the element of surprise. Or had he? "Red Two are you ready."

"Yes sir, everything's on-line."

"OK, activate now." As Pullman issued the order there was a load explosion near the edge of the crater. Remote controlled explosives, buried in the sand before they left, took out another Apache as it sat on the ground. Men scurried for cover, not sure where the explosion had come from.

As Pullman watched from his vantage point, he saw the last Apache and the Chinook start their engines and men leaping on board. Looks like they'd got the message. The Chinook would be all but defenceless on it's own, it appeared that whoever was in charge had come to the conclusion his best course of action was to retreat. The two helicopters, lifted away and headed back the way they'd come.

***

Shavit realised that he had been out-matched, for the moment. The Chinook would be a lumbering, almost defenceless target with only one Apache for support. "Everybody back to the helicopters," he shouted. One Apache would be no match for two, or maybe more, Puma's.

He punched the side of the Chinook in anger. He'd got a reputation in Mossad for completing a mission, but this time he'd badly misjudged the opposition. He'd known this was going to be a difficult mission and he'd been proven right.

"Have we lost any men?" he asked.

"Two Puma crews and three men on the ground when the explosives went off. Seven men altogether," replied his second-in-command.

"Damn!" the losses were too heavy to justify the minimal destruction he had achieved and now his opponents would be wary. He would have to answer some questions when he got back.

***

"OK, Red One keep radar surveillance on them. It doesn't matter if they see you on their radar now. Just make sure they keep going." Pullman allowed himself a smile, although the lack of markings on any of the helicopters, just like the jet, was worrying. It smelt of some sort of clandestine operation.

Pullman walked back to his waiting helicopter. "Open up a secure channel. I need to talk to someone. Red Three, go and pick up the civilians. Lets get this job finished as quickly as we can."

He put on the headphones passed to him by Corporal Johnson.

"OK sir, you're connected," confirmed Johnson.

"Captain John Pullman requesting contact with Field Marshall Wainwright, over."

"Wainwright here Pullman, good to hear from you." The Field Marshall and the Captain went way back. Pullman had served under him in Afghanistan just before the final pull-out and he knew how astute the Field Marshall was as a commanding officer.

"Thank you sir. We've had a bit of a situation here I thought you should be aware." He described the preceding events as concisely as he could.

"I see ... who would want to eliminate the site? I'm guessing whoever it was intercepted the emails and decided to pay you a call. You say they're returning the way they came." Wainwright was disturbed at the possible breach in security.

"Yes sir, could we put a satellite tail on them? I'd love to know where their heading." Pullman liked to know as much about his opponents as possible.

"Good idea, I'll organise it," confirmed Wainwright. "Do you think you'll be able to dig the civilians out?"

"Not sure sir, there's a lot of unstable sand. Still, we do have some well qualified people here. Hopefully we can gain access." Pullman wasn't really sure.

"OK, let me know if you need any extra support. In the meantime, keep watchful. Seems like you might have discovered something important to somebody," replied Wainwright. "Over and out."

By the time the civilians returned, Pullman's team had managed to clear away most of the remains of the burnt-out Apache and bury the bodies. Nothing had been found to help identify who had attacked them. The dead men hadn't carried any identification.

A few of the tents were torn but nothing that couldn't be patched up. His men were now assessing the damage to the crater, trying to decide how they could remove the sand-slide that obliterated the entrance to the Library. A short while later the civilian team joined them.

Chapter Eleven

In the Library

Mary had been heading back from the burial chamber to continue examining the rows of boxes when she heard a muffled explosion, then a noise like rain as the room went darker. The sunlight filtering through the part-open outer door stopped, a cloud of sand floated across the Library, settling in little eddies on the floor.

Si ran into the Library to find the door to the outside world blocked by a sand-drift, then another muffled explosion, this time a few fingers of sand fell from joints in the roof.

"Holy shit! Looks like the structure isn't stable or we've got another problem. I wonder if Pullman was right and there having more problems?" Si was worried.

"How are we going to get out of here? It'll take us days to dig that lot out and anyway we've only got our hands!" A hint of hysteria tinged Mary's voice.

She flashed the torch around the room and Si realised she was starting to panic. He wasn't filled with enthusiasm either at the thought of trying to dig their way out, but panicking wasn't going to help.

He put his hands on her shoulders, she was trembling. "Look at me! We ***will*** get out of here. I can't see that door being the only entrance to these buildings, there's bound to be another way out."

She stared into his face, her eyes wide in the dim torch light. "You don't understand, I hate enclosed spaces! I had a bad experience on one of my first digs when the side of the trench gave way and I got buried. It took three hours to dig me out! It's haunted me ever since."

Si pulled her to him and hugged her. "It'll be fine, trust me ... have you noticed the atmosphere in here wasn't musty when we first opened the Library. Perhaps there's fresh air getting in from somewhere?" Si sounded more hopeful than he felt. He tried the radio, but nothing. "Too much sand and rock to make contact."

"OK," Mary was trying to refocus, temporarily reassured by his embrace, "sorry for panicking ... you have a look around, see if you can find another door and I'll take as many photo's as I can of these tablets. I think I've started to crack the language." Mary wasn't going anywhere without as much information from the Library as possible and it would also stop her thinking about her fears.

Si glanced at the door and noticed that the sand was slowly drifting into the Library. The desert was trying to reclaim it's space and he knew there was no way they'd be able to shut the door to seal the gap. However, he kept his thoughts to himself and made a mental note to check how fast the sand was moving.

His first priority was to try and find another way out. If this room and the burial chamber were parts of a larger structure, then there must be other exits.

Checking that Mary was OK for the moment and engrossed in the tablets, he disappeared towards the back of the Library. He scanned the walls looking for any sign of another entrance to the room apart from the door to the burial chamber.

For the first time, he looked up at the roof and realised that it was constructed from stone blocks in the shape of a parabola.

He knew that the shape would mean the roof was self-supporting and would direct all of its weight directly down into the walls. He'd often used the idea at university to scam a drink out of any unsuspecting students by piling pennies in such a way that the top penny was overlapping passed the bottom penny, almost seeming to defy gravity.

Si noticed the beam from the torch dim slightly, a sign that the batteries were on their way out. Stuck in here without light would make finding an exit even more difficult, and goodness knows what it would do to Mary's state of mind.

He headed for the Burial Chamber to see if he could find anything in there.

Chapter Twelve

En route to Israel

Meir Shavit climbed back into the Chinook after the crew had refueled the two helicopters from drums they carried. "Open a channel to headquarters." This was a call he hadn't planned to make. "Shavit here, I'm afraid we've failed. There were armed forces protecting them. We've lost two helicopters, the F-15 and seven men."

Professor Claudio Borghese, the head of the Torah Cult listened intently. He'd assumed the position of leader only a few months before.

Born 1971 in Bologna as an only child, he had turned to the church when his parents were killed in a car accident, but had become disillusioned with the liberal attitude that was pervading the Catholic Church. He felt it was wrong and that the scandals of the past, child abuse, etc were unacceptable. So he'd stood down as one of the College of Cardinals and took a position in the Vatican University.

"Very disappointing Shavit, return to base. I thought that you were the right man for the job, I was obviously mistaken! Now we've also shown our hand making this even more difficult. I'll have to deal with this in a different way." This was the second time this year the cult had had to deal with an unwanted archeological find. This time, their plans had fallen apart. Level the site and bury any evidence, including any personnel they found. Should have been straight forward. Nobody would have found any trace in the middle of the Sahara. The landscape changed every time a sand storm blew across the surface. Now their efforts had been exposed. There were witnesses.

Fortunately, the cult was unknown. It had been set-up over 250 years ago to protect the established religions from sciences' continuous assaults on the Bible. When it was realised from various events, there was a possibility the Genesis story was just a story, the Torah Cult started monitoring any discoveries. Ever since then they had protected the Abrahamic religions, ensuring no evidence was exposed that could question their truth. Faith was getting harder to come by in today's materialistic society and people were only too keen to find ways to knock religion whenever an opportunity arose.

They couldn't try obliterating the site again. They'd just have to ensure any information that was published was not a threat. Professor Mary Freeman was going to wish she hadn't got involved.

Professor Borghese picked up the telephone, "Meira, I need your expertise."

Meira Heller was a Professor of History, a specialist in Pre-biblical studies in relation to the Jewish people. She worked at The Reuben and Edith Hecht Museum at the University of Haifa. The founder of the Museum, Dr. Hecht, who was known for his Zionist activities, believed archaeology was an important expression of Zionism and the discovery of ancient artefacts from the Canaanite period to the end of the Byzantine period were proof of the link between the Jewish people and the land of Israel.

"We have an information leak that needs to be stopped. The problem is a Professor Mary Freeman. Can you investigate?"

"Yes Claudio, I'll get on to it right away. Sooner we resolve the problem, the easier it will be." Meira had been recruited to the Torah Cult some years ago when her work supporting the history of the Jewish people had been published.

Meira put down the phone and started researching. Mary had been a challenging student and had resisted the accepted rules of academia; a number of relationships, one with one of her lecturers, her latest relationship breakdown leading to her escape to Timbuktu; controversial ideas on the origins of languages from a single unidentified root her entombment in a trench at Gobleki Tepe in Iran, the location of the worlds oldest discovered buildings and her lengthy recovery from the stress of being buried alive.

This was going to be easier than Meira had expected. She started to type an email to a respected archaeological journal questioning the validity of the information Mary had sent to Durham. Information that was now circulating academia via the Internet. She suggested Mary had falsified the information to regain respect with her colleagues. The images had clearly been created.

Meira then sent a copy to a contact in the international media.

Chapter Thirteen

A revelation

Si circled the second chamber looking for an exit. This time, there was no obvious door. The walls were smooth and the stone blocks fitted together precisely, each one carved to the exact shape necessary to interlock with its neighbours. He felt he'd seen this type of building before and remembered his visit to Machu Picchu when he was on his gap year from University.

He couldn't understand why the atmosphere in the building seemed so fresh. He was convinced there was some sort of ventilation system but he couldn't see any gaps in the walls. His attention finally turned to the strange stone troughs housing the ancient people.

He studied the crystal at the centre, leaned over the end of a trough and as he looked down, he noticed a dark shape in the floor. He pointed the torch and found a circular hole about a metre in diameter. Si struggled to get closer, hanging over the end of the trough, he saw what appeared to be foot holds cut into the sides and felt a coolness on his face.

"Mary ... Mary," he shouted. "I think I've found something."

He heard her jump down the steps in the Library. She appeared at the doorway, "what have you found?"

"I think it's a ventilation tunnel. I can feel air movement. It doesn't look easy to get to and it means a climb down into the dark but do you think you can manage it?" He hoped her desire to get out was greater than her claustrophobia.

"I'm not sure. Isn't there any other way?" She didn't like the idea of the dark shaft at all.

"Can't find anything else. I've searched every inch of the walls and there doesn't appear to be anything, not even a crack," he replied.

"Why don't you take a look? I got a few more tablets to photograph and, if it isn't a way out, I won't have to brave the dark," Mary smiled unconvincingly.

"If you're sure you'll be alright," though he wasn't sure about anything. She nodded and went back into the Library.

Si climbed over the trough and crouched above the shaft, the crystal suspended inches above his head. He shone the torch down and saw a tunnel running horizontally across the bottom about two metres down. He squeezed past the crystal and sat on the edge, found a foot hold and lowered himself down. Braced against the side of the shaft, he felt for each protrusion. After a few minutes he reached the bottom. The tunnel was about a metre high and disappeared into the darkness in both directions.

As he crouched there pondering which way to go, he felt a slight breeze coming from one of the tunnels. Deciding that was their best chance, he crawled along.

After about ten metres, he sensed the tunnel roof disappear. He pointed the flash-light upwards and found himself below another short vertical shaft. Standing up, his head was just above the rim of the floor. He swept the torch around the room and was astonished to see a man sitting on a stone block in the centre. He was dressed as a Tuareg and appeared strangely familiar. Si realised it was the same man they had met in the bar.

"How on earth did you get here?" Si exclaimed.

"I came to help you," came the reply. "Your journey is not yet complete."

"What do you mean ... who are you?" Si was confused.

"I am Lucere of the Orbiane. We lived here many centuries ago and co-existed with your people. We have been waiting for your civilisation to mature, so we can continue to pass on the knowledge we had developed over many thousands of years. This place is one of the locations around the world where we have stored our knowledge for you. We believe it is now time to expose you to the truth." He spoke in a deep sonorous voice that echoed around the chamber.

"I don't understand. You say you lived here alongside us many years ago ... but you look like us?" Si was finding it difficult to understand.

"I have materialised in a form that would not be threatening to you. We developed the ability to transcend our physical bodies and to exist as energy. We are all around you, and one day you will develop the ability to see us again. The remains of our original shape lie in the transcender tubes you have just been studying," explained Lucere. "We have tried revealing our secrets before, but some amongst you do not want the truth of your history to be revealed. In order to reveal this site to you we altered the orbit of the asteroid."

"You altered the orbit ... ! so that explains what happened," not that it really explained anything. Si thought back to Robin's comment about the electromagnetic pulse that was detected but, for the moment, Si was more concerned about getting out, explanations could come later. "If we can't get out of here, your efforts will have been for nothing." The pieces were slowly starting to come together. Someone was trying to hide the Library. "Is there another way out?"

"Yes, there is another way. I will show you, but first your companion must collect as much information as she can. It is important this site is revealed. Our remaining sites are now lost under many fathoms of water and will be much more difficult for you to explore."

Si was puzzled, "how old is your civilisation?"

"We walked the earth more than 100,000 years ago before the last ice time. That was when our civilisation inhabited large areas of the earth. However, our cities were either destroyed by the ice or submerged when the sea levels rose following the thaw. Your myths call it the Great Flood. We have been waiting to pass on our knowledge but the religious bigotry of the last two thousand years has meant we had to wait for a more enlightened time. We believe that time is now," Lucere explained.

"You keep saying we ... how many of you are there?"

"We are many," and as Lucere spoke, orbs of light swirled around him. Si's mind was filled with images of great cities with tall slender people. There were humans, mingled amongst them, showing no fear.

"*This is the way we communicate with you,*" Si could hear the voice, but Lucere was not speaking. "*We have communicated with many people over time. You feel our communication as revelations, spirits, brain-waves, inspiration, dreams, even ghosts. You have created many words to describe these feelings. We have helped civilisations achieve a great status before, like the Mayans and the Egyptians."*

"So that's where their knowledge started!" Si had studied the Mayans and their strange calendar and had wondered how such an advanced civilisation could suddenly appear from nowhere.

"*We discovered the way to liberate our bodies. The chamber you were exploring is the place where we merged our spirit with the planet's life force. The crystal channelled the earth's energy, unfortunately, the ground has moved and it's no longer connected to its energy source."*

Si had been so engrossed in the story he had momentarily forgotten about Mary. "I need to go and fetch my companion. You say there's a way out ... where should we go?"

"Bring your companion here. I will show you the way," said Lucere.

Chapter Fourteen

Escape

Si slipped back into the tunnel and crawled as quickly as he could to the room containing the transcender tubes. As he got closer, he heard Mary's voice echoing down the tunnel shouting his name. He called back and climbed up the shaft to find her leaning over with a look of panic.

"Where have you been!" Tears ran down her face leaving little rivers of sand on her cheeks. "I've been calling for ten minutes, I thought you'd got trapped or something worse! I told you I can't stand enclosed spaces for long!"

"It's OK, calm down. There's a way out, although you won't believe how I know." Si quickly described his encounter with Lucere, the purpose of the Libraries and the deflection of the asteroid.

Mary's eyes grew wider, her tears stopped. "That's amazing, you're sure you didn't bump your head in the tunnel and dream all of this?" Even she was finding it difficult to believe.

"I did have to pinch myself a few times," Si smiled. "Have you got the information you need?"

"Yes, I've taken as many photo's as the camera can hold. Now, get me out of here before I start screaming again!"

Si dropped down the shaft and held the torch for Mary to see the foot holds. "Careful how you climb over, the shaft isn't too bad to get down. Just have to mind your head in the tunnel. Lucere said meet him back in the other room." They both crawled along the tunnel, Mary held onto one of Si's boots and tried not to think of the tons of sand and stone a few inches above her head.

When they climbed out into the next room Lucere was still sitting on the stone block. He smiled as they entered. Mary recognised him from the bar, the same haunting eyes.

"Welcome. Have you gathered the information you need?" asked Lucere.

"I've taken pictures of as many tablets as I can ... Si told me about your conversation. He said you know of another way out."

Lucere stood up and walked over to the far side of the room and placed his right hand on a circular stone built into the wall. A slight glow flashed from his fingertips and a section of the wall moved backwards.

"The mechanisms are powered by sand," Lucere explained. "A slight movement in the stone causes the sand to flow into pendulums that swing and release the door." He stepped through the opening. "We created this system to protect our knowledge until you were ready. We buried the buildings beneath the desert to preserve them. We used the asteroid to expose the entrance."

Si and Mary followed Lucere and found themselves in a long arched gallery. The floor was polished stone and it was difficult to identify any cracks between the blocks. The walls were a similar interlocking structure to the other rooms they'd seen. The roof was the same parabolic shape as the Library, but on a smaller scale.

"How did you manage to deflect the asteroid?" Si was puzzled.

"It was very difficult for us. To cause a physical change takes much of our energy. We had to focus all our resources and we can only maintain the effort for a very short time. Fortunately, it was enough. However, we did lose some of our people in the process," Lucere's voice trembled. "Because of this, it is important our efforts are not in vain. Our knowledge must be released so you can take your final steps to a peaceful civilisation."

"Si tells me your civilisation is incredibly ancient. Why don't we know more about you?" Mary was puzzled.

"You do know. You just don't believe. We exist in all of your societies' myths. We are known by many names; Viaracocha, Quetzalcoatl, Bochica, Votan of American peoples, the gods of the Greeks, Romans, Indians, Inuits, Osiris of the Egyptians. There are many," recounted Lucere.

"Were you the legend that the Aztec's were looking for when the Spanish arrived?" asked Mary.

"Unfortunately that is true. We co-existed with humans and you treated us as near gods. Our intelligence and abilities were beyond you then as you were hunter gatherers. We guided you as best we could, teaching you fire, helping you to refine tools and teaching you about crops to reduce your dependency on killing animals for food."

"Why did you do all this?" queried Mary.

"We felt protective of you as if you were our children. Although our origins are the same, we evolved much earlier," Lucere explained as they walked down the gallery. "You also helped us to create some of our cities. You were physically stronger and more dexterous. In return, we taught you to build boats, to navigate large stretches of water. You were a willing labour force and with our help you were able to expand into areas where food was plentiful. It was a symbiotic relationship."

Mary noticed many carvings in alcoves along the walls. Some were statues of the Orbianes, some were human and in some alcoves there were paintings and diagrams.

"Are you the civilisation that mapped the earth before Antarctica moved position?" Mary was getting excited as she realised the riddle of ancient world maps may finally be solved.

"Yes. All of this was created to educate you about our civilisation and how you have evolved, so you can understand your place in the universe." Lucere waved his hands at the various artefacts as they passed.

"What about the Pyramids in Egypt? Did you build those?" Mary was starting to understand the scope of the Orbiane world.

"Yes, they were our first attempts at trying to understand the energy inherent in everything, including the energy we receive from the universe."

"So that's why there is no evidence from Egyptian history about how the Pyramids were constructed. Their defining image isn't theirs at all! The Egyptians didn't construct them, just used what was already there for their own purposes." Mary had just answered a riddle she, and many others, had struggled with for years.

"The Egyptians were the labour force we used for their construction but, at that time, they had no written language to record the methods we used," explained Lucere.

"Why did your civilisation come to an end?" Lucere was describing a powerful race, but Mary knew no evidence had been found.

"In our cities, we developed technology to harness the energy of the earth. We had a focal point in the centre of our cities that channelled the energy from the earth and the sun into heat or light as required. This was too advanced for you to understand. You thought it was power from the gods. But just like you are today, we suffered a change in the climate. As the world progressed into the ice-age, some of the cities were engulfed by ice. We abandoned those places and our people moved to cities closer to the equator. This upset the delicate balance between our energy needs and the energy available. Some of our people started to die from lack of sustenance." Lucere sounded sad as he recalled the death throes of his earthly civilisation.

"But why haven't we found any evidence?" As an archaeologist, Mary couldn't accept that nothing was left from such a widespread, advanced civilisation.

"The ice eroded all evidence of our civilisation on higher land. The few cities left around the equator were built near the sea and when the ice-age ended, the sea levels rose flooding the last few cities. In time, you will find other artefacts, particularly under the seas. Think how much of the earth's surface you have examined. There is much more to explore."

"It's true, we've only looked at a tiny percentage, and if we have to include the sea beds, then we've hardly explored anything."

"A few cities remained like this one in the Sahara, but we realised our time was at an end. So we concealed the last three which were spaced around the world, here in the Sahara, the jungles of Ecuador and the centre of Australia. When the time was right, we would reveal their presence to you. We feel that now the time is right." Lucere was reliving the memories of those distant times.

"I see, so there are other sites to find?" asked Mary.

"There are, but the city in Ecuador has been destroyed. The people who attacked you here, succeeded in hiding the discovery in Ecuador. They obliterated the site with explosives and burnt the jungle." Lucere had a hint of anger in his tone.

"So that's what the fire was about in Ecuador. I lost a friend in that fire, she had gone there to search for evidence of hidden cities in the jungle." Mary was also feeling angry. "Why didn't you stop these people?"

"The Torah Cult, as they are called, are so bigoted their minds are closed to our communications. We can only encourage change through communication with open minds," repeated Lucere.

"So after you hid the cities, what happened?" asked Mary.

"We used a method we had been developing to transform our physical bodies into light energy. It was very unpredictable at the time, but we felt we had no choice. Some of my people died trying to perfect the method, but we finally managed to transform most of our population from the room you found."

"And you've existed as energy since then?" Mary was finding this difficult to comprehend.

"Yes, do you remember when you were buried, did anything strange happen while they were trying to find you?" asked Lucere.

"After about an hour, the digging stopped and I thought that they'd given up trying to find me. I was about to give up hope when an image flashed into my mind. I was on a stage, years into the future, giving a lecture. I didn't know what the subject was, but in that instant, I knew that I was going to get out."

Lucere smiled and looked deep into her eyes, for a second the image of the stage filled her mind. "You mean, that was you?"

"Not me, but one of us who was looking after you. We knew you were going to be part of this discovery. It was important that you survived. All through the ages we have help and guided those of you who are receptive, guiding you to develop an awareness of your place in the universe. The path isn't easy and some get side-tracked, others are so fearful of change they will destroy to keep the truth hidden." Lucere stopped as they reached the end of the gallery.

He pressed the wall and exposed a doorway. A warm breeze drifted through. Si saw a cliff face with steps cut into the rock, sunlight streamed from somewhere high above.

"Those steps will lead you out. You have been chosen to expose the truth, but it will not be easy. Many forces are at work against you. You will need courage. I will leave you now, but if you need help again, I will be near." With those words, Lucere expanded into a flash of light which condensed into a small orb and shot skywards.

Chapter Fifteen

Out at last

Si and Mary looked at each other, trying to assess how each was going to react.

Mary was the first to speak, "I find this so difficult to believe, yet on another level I know it's the truth!"

"It's certainly beyond my sphere of expertise, but I do believe what we've just been told," agreed Si. "Mind you, who is going to believe us? Unless we can show this site to the world, we've got nothing except some crazy ideas."

"Well, let's get up these steps and see what's been happening," said Mary as she started to climb.

The steps were cut in a zigzag that climbed high above their heads. The rock face was protected by a stone wall that had been constructed like a chimney. As they climbed higher the sunlight grew brighter until, after an exhausting climb of about two hundred feet, they emerged onto a high rock ledge overlooking the crater.

Mary turned to Si as he stepped out and held him tight. Tears of emotion rolled down her cheeks. She whispered in his ear, "thanks for keeping me calm, I guess you were just as worried as I was."

"I've had better days, I must admit," Si assured her.

They gazed down on the crater and saw how the edge had collapsed above the library entrance, completely obliterating it. At this distance in the heat of the overhead sun, it was difficult to make out any detail. The remains of a helicopter were smoking in a small crater not far from their camp. In the distance they could see another column of smoke rising from behind a sand dune.

Si cupped his hands to his eyes to cut out the glare and focus on the camp. As his eyes adjusted, he made out a few people scurrying around. A small group were at the edge of the crater where the platform used to be. The sound of a helicopter broke the silence as it rose over a sand dune heading for the camp. It landed near the wreckage of a helicopter and people climbed out.

"I think those are our people ... do you think the camp is safe?" asked Si.

"There isn't any sign of fighting now. Seems pretty calm, try Pullman on the radio, it should work now," suggested Mary.

"Good idea ... Pullman, are you there?"

After a long few minutes, the radio burst into life. "Hey ... where are you ... are you both OK, over?" The sound of Pullman's voice was reassuring.

"Yes, we're both fine. We're on a ridge to the east looking down at you," Si waved.

Pullman looked through his binoculars at the ridge where the Puma had sat a few hours before and saw Si and Mary waving.

"Glad to see you back, hold on, I'll send a chopper." Pullman turned to one of his men and issued the order.

Ten minutes later, Si and Mary were sitting at the long camp table describing the events that had taken place underground.

"If I didn't know you better, I'd say you were both crazy! Underground cities, light beings, ancient cults! When I first saw that doorway in the side of the crater, I knew this was going to be a 'different' kind of mission." Pullman smiled, "but it does give us a better idea of who's trying to stop us."

Pullman described the events that happened above ground.

"Someone sounds pretty serious, was anybody injured?" asked Si.

"Luckily, no, although I can't vouch for the other side. Whoever they are, they've got some pretty hefty money behind them. To keep that sort of operation secret, they must have important connections in some country or other."

Chapter Sixteen

Outrage

"Mary, I think you should come and see this!" shouted Charlie, the Technical Secretary, from under the canopy. She had been browsing the Internet looking for any feedback on the images that had been transmitted to Durham.

Mary stood behind her to read the screen. She felt her face flush and the anger build inside. "What the hell is going on? Who is Professor Meira Heller? Si, come and look at this. I think we know what Lucere was referring to."

Si walked over and read the screen. "So that's the next game. Discredit you, so that anything you publish will be ignored. They couldn't destroy the site, so they're going to destroy you!" Si was starting to appreciate the scale of the problem. "It's no good transmitting any more pictures at the moment, they'll only be discredited. We need some physical evidence to show to the world."

"Well, at least we know another way in to the Library. We can retrieve some of those tablets and get them to the UK for carbon dating ... Pullman, can you get us back up to that ridge?" Mary was determined to recover her reputation.

"No problem, we can keep a watch on the radar as well, just in case we have any more surprise visits. The 'Torah Cult' seem very determined and well connected," Pullman didn't want to take any chances

"I'd like to see inside this place. I'm interested in how they managed to create a structure that's lasted so long. Will you need any help?" asked Tom Gardiner, the Mining Engineer.

"Help's always useful Tom, and you might see the structure from a different perspective than me and Mary," remarked Si. "Let's get started. The sooner we can disprove these statements, the better."

"The helicopter should be ready in about five minutes ... see you there." Pullman left to organise the movement.

"Let's hope those doors are still open. Otherwise, we'll have another problem." Si pondered. "Right, let's get going."

The three civilians walked over to the helicopter that was idling on the edge of the camp. Si helped Mary into the side door and climbed in, Tom followed. Minutes later, the helicopter dropped onto the ridge where they'd stood earlier.

They climbed out and were lowered down to the ledge four metres below by the SAS soldiers. In the face of the rock was the split through which they had emerged, angled so it would be impossible to tell from a distance that it disappeared inside the outcrop. Si went through first, followed by Mary and Tom. Si flicked on the torch to reveal the top of the chimney construction protecting the steps. Tom was immediately engrossed in the construction of the stones.

"This is amazing ... the accuracy of the carving ... smoothness of the stone! When did you say this was built?" Tom couldn't believe his eyes.

"Lucere said it was about 100,000 years old," replied Mary.

"It seems impossible. I'm not surprised they're managing to discredit you. It's contrary to all we know of the capabilities of very ancient peoples," said Tom.

"That's why we need to get some physical evidence, to prove the dates ... let's get down there." Mary wanted to get started.

Si led the way to the top of the steps. "Be careful, some sand has drifted in and made them quite slippery in places."

They started to descend using flash-lights to pick out the steps. Half way down, Mary's foot slipped on the sand. She instinctively reached out to regain her balance, grabbing the back of Si's jacket. He turned to steady her, "we'll get there, no need to take the quick way down!"

Mary took a deep breath and continued her descent, checking her grip as she went.

Progress was slow and when they eventually reached the bottom they saw that the doorway through which they had come a few hours earlier was still open. They slipped through into the long gallery.

Tom scanned the structure with his torch, "this is amazing, the accuracy of the stone work, the carvings, it can't possibly be that old!"

They reached the end of the gallery to find the door closed. Si scanned the wall. "Lucere touched a round stone in the face of the wall. Can you see anything like that?"

They each searched a part of the wall but couldn't find anything that looked like the release stone.

"Maybe it's different on this side," said Si. "Look for anything."

"What's this?" Mary shouted. She had been looking on the side wall of the gallery and found a hand sized hole. "Do you think this could be it?"

She shone the light down the cavity. It was about half a metre deep, and at the end she could see what looked like a handle carved into the stone. "I've don't like the look of this. Let's check the door again, look for any symbols."

They searched the surfaces again, but couldn't find anything that might help.

"We'll just have to try it." Mary plunged her arm into the hole and gripped the handle. "I don't know which way it moves, but I can't make it do anything."

"Let me try," volunteered Tom. Mary withdrew her arm and Tom pushed in his. "It's quiet tight around my arm, I can just reach." His face flushed as he struggled to move the handle. "I think it's turning."

A grating noise could be heard from inside the wall, and the door slowly slid open.

"Well done Tom," cried Mary. "Let's get going."

"Wait! I can't get my arm out! As the door opened, a stone in the wall has moved and locked my hand in." Tom pulled back, but with no success. His arm was held fast. "Maybe if I turn the handle back it will release my arm?"

"Can you hold on? If we close the door it may not open again. We can go and get the evidence and then try and release your arm when we get back." Mary was desperate to get to the Library.

"Mary, you can't be serious. Tom's stuck. Surely we should sort him out first!"

"It's OK, Mary's right. You go and get the stuff. But please, be as quick as you can, I can start to feel my arm going numb!" said Tom.

"But we might not have time! If your arm isn't released when we close the door, we'll have to try and smash a hole into the wall. We'll need to go back and get tools, by the time we've got you out, you could have lost your arm. Don't you see the risks!" Si looked from one to the the other for a glimpse of agreement.

"Come on, Tom's decided, let's get a move on." Mary dived through the door, not waiting for an argument.

Si was seeing a side of Mary he hadn't seen before, and wasn't sure he liked. Frowning, he followed her into the strange circular room. They rushed over to the ventilation hole and jumped down, quickly crawled along the tunnel and climbed into the Transcender Room. Mary struggled over a stone trough, crushing the skeleton's remains in her haste. Si was more nimble, dropped to the floor and followed her through into the Library.

"Which ones are you going to choose?" asked Si.

"I think I should take one from each level. They get more complex as they get higher. You hold them and I'll pull them out." Si forced the lids and lifted out examples. Soon, Mary's outstretched arms were sagging supporting the ancient delicate amber sheets.

After selecting ten sheets, they dropped down the steps and headed for the tunnel. Manoeuvring the delicate sheets over the troughs, down into the tunnels and out to where Tom was captive, was a slow process.

They rushed into the gallery to see Tom sagging.

"My arms almost completely dead. I'm not sure I've got the strength to turn the stone!" Tom sounded desperate.

"Try pumping your hand to get the blood flowing before you try," suggested Si.

Tom grimaced and put all of his determination into moving the handle. After what was an agonising few minutes, the grating sound was heard again. The door slowly closed behind them and Tom managed to withdraw his arm from the hole. He rubbed an area around his wrist where deep red patches were slowly turning blue.

"Not sure I fancy doing that again! Reminded me of one of those fortune telling faces you get in fun-fairs where you put your hand in their mouth. Never did like them!" Tom smiled, glad to have his arm back. "At least you got the tablets."

"Glad your OK Tom ... and thanks. Are you happy you came along?" asked Mary.

"Wouldn't have missed this for the world, something to tell the grandchildren. What an amazing structure this is!" Tom gazed around the gallery in awe.

"Let's get the evidence to the world. Are you OK carrying those tablets?" Mary asked Si.

"Sure, there not heavy, just delicate. Come on." Si started walking quickly down the gallery.

They reached the bottom of the steps and started to climb. Progress was slow with Si trying to hold the tablets and also balance up the narrow steps They eventually reached the top and emerged onto the ledge. The SAS men had already lowered a collapsible ladder. Si passed them the tablets and they climbed up to the helicopter and were transported back to camp.

Mary laid out the tablets on the table and everyone gathered round. Pullman was the first to make a comment. "They're amazing, and you believe they maybe as old as 100,000 years! Wow!"

Si was the first to notice. "Mary, have you seen the writing, it's fading in the sunlight and the tablets seem to be softening and losing their shape!"

Mary lifted one of the tablets, which bent as if it was a thin plastic film. She examined the writing, "damn, they can't take exposure to this level of heat and light ... of course, the climate wasn't so extreme here when they were first placed in the Library. Quick, cover them up ... have we got a fridge or freezer?" She looked at Pullman.

"Not here," Pullman's practical brain went into overdrive. "What if we put them into a container and squirt in a Fire-extinguisher?"

Mary looked puzzled, but Si understood. "Brilliant, the CO_2 from the extinguisher will cool the interior as it condenses. Should work as long as we top it up occasionally."

Pullman turned to one of his men. "Grab one of those empty missiles containers and bring it over here with a fire extinguisher as quick as you can." The soldier raced to the lead helicopter. "The container should be just the right size."

By the time the tablets had been loaded into the container, they were quite soft and half the writing had disappeared. The CO_2 was injected and the lid sealed. A slight hoar frost formed around the container.

"We're going to have to fetch some more tablets," said Mary. "We can't be sure these will last the journey to England. We could seal them into a container while we're in the Library before we bring them up to the surface."

"Well, I'm not opening the door," smiled Tom, rubbing his arm.

"Nor me, we'll have to find another way to turn the handle ... Pullman, we need another idea, something to turn a handle, about half a metre away," said Si. He described the door mechanism.

"Shouldn't be too difficult. We've got some tube left over from the platform." Pullman's ability to solve a problem quickly had saved his life many times. During his two tours of duty in Afghanistan, he was awarded the Conspicuous Gallantry Cross for attacking a Taliban stronghold with minimal back-up and a lot of ingenuity, capturing the Taliban Military Commander in the process.

Pullman glanced at the sky, "it'll be sunset in about an hour. I think it'd be wise to go down the shaft in the morning. If something goes wrong, we don't want to be thrashing about in the dark."

"But what if the Torah Cult return? I need to get those tablets out. Surely we've got enough time?" Mary didn't want to risk losing the artefacts she needed to clear her name.

"I'm sorry, Mary, It's my job to look after your safety and I think it's a bad idea to carry on now." Pullman was quite firm.

"You've kept us safe so far," said Si, "I'll trust your judgement. Come on Mary, we've got plenty of photo's to go through. Let's see if we can make any progress with the language."

Si and Mary were up most of the night, trawling through the photo's. They started to compile a dictionary of the language. As their understanding developed, Mary could see how the text had influences in other ancient languages.

"This text reminds me of Vedic Sanskrit, one of the oldest written languages, probably three to four thousand years old; the root of many modern languages. But this seems to me to be more like the foundation of Sanskrit. If it is, it means current written languages were based on this ancient civilisation." She smiled. This would vindicate one of her theories.

Everyone else were in their tents trying to get some rest before the early morning start. Neither Mary nor Si felt tired, adrenalin coursed through their veins following the excitement of the day.

She turned to Si, "you've been a wonderful support to me, I'm very grateful you let me come along and take over your expedition."

"Si placed his hand on Mary's arm and gently squeezed. I'm glad you came along. Studying some asteroid wouldn't have been half as exciting as the fun we've had." Si laughed, "what's between you and Pullman?"

"Me and Pullman?" Mary was surprised by the question. "Oh, we had a moment when I first arrived, he's a sensitive man when you get under his professional exterior. But it didn't last long, now we're just good friends ... why do you ask?"

"You two seem very close, I just thought there might be something more to it ... only, I enjoy your company and I don't really want it to end when this is over." Si found it hard trying to express his feelings.

Mary leant closer as she whispered, "I feel the same. I've had some history to get over, but, in a strange way, I think you've helped me through that."

Si closed the gap and kissed her. She responded with a passion. "My tent's closer than yours," she whispered.

Chapter Seventeen

Tuesday 17th April 2029

As the sun rose, the camp burst into activity. Si slipped out of Mary's tent hoping they hadn't disturbed anyone in the night. He grabbed his wash bag and towel from his tent and made for the temporary shower.

He met Pullman who was on the way back. "Have a good night?" Pullman smiled. "We should be ready in about half an hour. I'm loading a few extra bits and pieces that might help when we get up there."

Si thanked him and pressed on to the shower.

Mary stretched in her sleeping bag and smiled. She realised her feelings for Si were quite different to any other relationship she'd had. She pulled on the white kaftan that Pullman had given her when she first arrived in Timbuktu, left her tent and headed for the shower.

Si was in the canvas shower. Mary found herself just listening to the noises he made when suddenly the zip shot up and he emerged wrapped in a towel. He slipped past, gave her a quick kiss and before she had time to say anything, he was gone.

They met Pullman at the helicopter. "I'll get the camp packed away while you're down there. We can head back to Timbuktu as soon as you've recovered what you need. Two of my men will come with you to help you bring out the artefacts ... good luck!"

They climbed into the helicopter, it lifted immediately and headed for the rock outcrop.

As the helicopter settled, the two soldiers jumped out and helped Mary and Si onto the uneven surface. Then they unloaded a couple of rucksacks, from one, a long pole protruded, hopefully the 'key' to the door.

Si led the way with Mary close behind, followed by the two soldiers. They cautiously descended the stone staircase and came to the open outer door. They passed down the gallery to the second door, which was closed as before. Si found the hole and guided in the pole to grip either side of the handle. One of the soldiers grabbed the t-piece welded across the end, and turned.

The grating noise started and the door slowly slid open. They left the pole in place holding the handle and passed through. Retracing their steps through the now familiar tunnels, they emerged into the library. Gasps of astonishment accompanied the two soldiers.

Mary rushed up the steps and selected a box she had examined the previous day. She now knew, based on their research, the contents described some of the events of the dying days of the Orbiane civilisation.

The two soldiers pulled some 'gaffer' tape out of a rucksack and proceeded to seal the lid of the copper box, inserting a small rubber tube into the corner. They taped a fire extinguisher to the top and connected the hose.

The box was then lifted and carried to the room containing the transcender tubes, carefully lowered down the shaft, and out into the circular room; back through the doorway where Si grabbed the tube from the hole after closing the door. The four then quickly passed down the gallery to the foot of the steps.

A wire cable hung near the bottom step. The winch-man from the helicopter had lowered the cable into the shaft while they were collecting the box. The cable was attached and, following radio instructions from one of the soldiers, the box was slowly winched up as they ascended the stairs, making sure the precious box didn't snag on any of the steps.

At the top, the box was carefully placed in the helicopter. Si flicked open the fire-extinguisher for a few seconds to keep the contents cool, the helicopter lifted off and made for the camp.

Although they had been gone less than an hour, Pullman had packed everything away.

The helicopter landed and picked up the rest of the civilians and soldiers. The three helicopters rose into the air and headed back south, skimming the seemingly unending sand dunes as they headed towards the SAS camp.

A couple of hours later, the Pumas dropped onto the tarmac of the SAS base. The civilians climbed into a waiting Ocelot transporter, configured for passengers, to deliver them to Timbuktu airfield. Pullman instructed his men to store the box in the camp cold room. Turning to the waiting Ocelot, Pullman shouted, "take the civilians to the airfield. We'll bring these two later, there's a few things to sort out." He turned back to Mary, "I'll see what transport I can organise to get you back. You say you want to get to Durham?"

"Yes, we've got all the equipment we need at Durham to analyse the tablets and I know and trust all the people." Mary realised other institutions might not be too co-operative following her character assassination on the internet.

"OK, I'll give you a call as soon as I've got things sorted. One of my men will drop you back at the airstrip." Pullman turned and headed for the communications block.

"Let's get back to Timbuktu and get packed," said Mary.

They followed the soldier to another Ocelot and climbed aboard. The soldier dropped them at the airstrip. Mary jumped into her vehicle and Si climbed in beside her.

He realised this was the first time they'd been alone since the start of the expedition. A lot had happened in a short time and Si was starting to feel a deep bond developing between them, he wondered if Mary felt the same.

They made the journey in silence, although, occasionally, Mary would glance across at him and smile.

They stopped at Mary's first to pick up few belongings, but as soon as they arrived, they knew something was wrong. The door to the small building she rented had been forced open and hung at an angle from it's broken hinges.

Si held Mary's arm to stop her rushing in. "Let's take it steady, we don't want to walk into a trap." He whispered and edged up to the door to listen. No sound, he peered around the door frame, but couldn't see anything in the dim light. He felt Mary close behind.

As his eyes became accustomed to the half-light, he could see the room was in shambles. Papers and furniture scattered across the floor.

"Whoever has done this has gone," said Mary as she pushed past Si and entered the room. He tried to grab her as she went past. He was sure he'd seen a movement, just a momentary glimpse out of the corner of his eye, but it was too late. A dark shape lunged forward and grabbed her. Si could see the glint of a pistol being held to her head.

"Come inside where I can see you, or I'll shoot her and then you!" A thickly accented voice shouted out.

Si stepped into the dim room.

"Pick-up those chairs! Quickly!" the voice commanded. "Now sit on them".

They sat down, unsure what was going to happen. The man moved behind them, grabbed their wrists, pulled them under the chairs and tied them with cable ties. They both sat hunched forward, chest on their thighs, unable to move or even look up.

"Now, tell me what you plan to do. Have you removed any evidence from the site?" The voice was cold. Si was trying to place the accent, maybe Italian?

"What do you want?" Mary sounded defiant.

The kidnapper swung his gun and hit her across the face. Her cheek split and started to bleed. Si struggled, trying to move, but it was no good.

"Answer my questions, or I'll kill you now!" the intruder demanded.

Si saw the man's feet, expensive Italian shoes? He felt cold metal on the back of his neck. "I'll kill your friend if you don't answer!"

"You'll kill us anyway," shouted Si.

"Maybe, maybe not, that's the chance you've got to take ... answer the question," he demanded.

"Why do you care what we've found?" Mary could feel her anger rise with the hopelessness of the situation.

"I have friends who need some answers. You've no idea who you are dealing with. If you did, you would answer the question." The man sounded as if he was loosing his patience.

"Fuck you and your friends," she shouted.

Blat, a gun shot filled the room, Mary screamed, sure her careless words had signed Si's death warrant. A body collapsed in front of her. The first man that she'd been attracted to for a long time was lying at her feet because of her stubbornness. She couldn't bear to look. Then she heard a noise coming from the direction of the doorway.

"Are you both OK?" a familiar voice asked.

Mary felt her hands being freed. She sat up to see a man dressed in a dark coat lying at her feet, a pool of blood slowly forming beneath his head. She glanced across to the other chair where Pullman was now releasing Si.

Mary's heart leapt. She realised she'd have been devastated if Si had been shot, her impetuousness had nearly got them both killed. "Am I glad to see you!" she said, "what are you doing here?"

"I went to the Radio room to sort out transport, and one of my men said there'd been someone suspicious asking questions in the bars trying to find out where you lived. I put two and two together and thought it might be a good idea to check you were OK. When I got here, I heard the commotion."

"Who are these people?" said Mary.

While they were talking, Pullman was going through the gunman's pockets. He pulled out a passport, a cellphone and an empty wallet. "I expect the Passport's phoney, but the cellphone might help. There might be a number on here we can use. Let's get back to base. At least I can protect you there. Oh ... we should be getting the transport to the UK in a few hours."

Back at the SAS base, Pullman gave the phone to his Communications Officer, with instructions to check the numbers to see to whom they were registered.

Ten minutes later the Comms Officer joined them in the Canteen where they were having a cold beer. "Two of the numbers are pay-as-you-go phones, no names are registered. The third number is the home number of Yossi Marzan. I checked him out, he's thought to work for Mossad as a freelance agent."

"I thought this had the smell of Mossad," said Pullman. "We've been lucky so far. They don't normally screw-up. We need to be extra vigilant, they don't give-up either." Pullman had a bad feeling ever since the unmarked F-15 made it's appearance.

"What is Mossad?" Mary had heard the name, but had no idea what they did.

"They're the Institute for Intelligence and Special Operations. They've been appointed by the State of Israel to collect information, analyse intelligence, and perform special covert operations beyond its borders. But why they're bothered about an archaeological site is a mystery. Unless they've been hired by someone with a lot of influence." Pullman couldn't work out why anyone would be so keen to prevent the site from being discovered.

Chapter Eighteen

The journey home

"You know you don't have to come with me. If Pullman's right it looks like it could be dangerous," said Mary. She didn't want to get Si more involved than he was.

She'd recovered a few of her belongings and they were en-route to Si's hotel. The transport Pullman had arranged was due at the airstrip in an hour.

"You don't think I'm going to leave you to get all the glory for this discovery!" Si winked. "Besides, I'm rather enjoying your company."

Inwardly she was grateful to have him with her and not just for the company. They pulled up outside the hotel and Si went in to settle his bill and collect his bag. While he was inside, Mary thought back over the events of the last few days and realised her attraction to him had started in London when they had first met. She'd enjoyed his good humour and his positive outlook on life; very little seemed to get him down.

He emerged, bag over his shoulder, thrust it into the back of the Land Rover, jumped in beside her and they drove off in the direction of the airstrip.

The other civilians were waiting there for the flight back to the UK and the Marines were assembling the equipment back onto pallets to wait for the C-133 to return.

Pullman had intimated their transport might be a bit unusual. His Chief had pulled a few strings in order to get them out of Africa as quickly as possible. As they waited outside the terminal building in the shade of the late afternoon sun, a high pitched whisper approached. They looked to the north and saw a small black aircraft materialise through the heat haze. It shot over the airstrip, circled and dropped gracefully onto the tarmac.

Si couldn't believe his eyes. As it approached the buildings he got a clearer view. Stood on the runway was a very strange looking aircraft. The size of an executive jet, it was jet black and it looked as if it was made from glass. No obvious windows and the fuselage shape was reminiscent of a boat, rectangular in cross-section, coming to a 'bow shape' at the front. The wings looked as if some giant hand had pinched the sides and stretched them out like elastic, leaving them to set. The tailplane, in the shape of a scimitar, was set high on the rudder, with two jet engines mounted either side.

He turned to Mary, "I've never seen anything like it!"

As he spoke, a panel in the side opened and the pilot stepped down. He strolled over to Mary and Si. "I'm Captain John Crowther, are you Professor Simon Cartwright?"

"That's me, this is Professor Mary Freeman ... what on earth is that!?" asked Si.

"It's an experimental Rutan design that NASA has been evaluating. It's the first aircraft made entirely from carbon fibre; very light and strong. It can cruise at 70,000 feet at a speed of 600 miles per hour, just below the speed of sound, and has a range of 6,000 miles. It's almost radar invisible, got a special transponder that broadcasts a radar image so Air Traffic Control can see the aircraft."

"Wow ... where have you come from?" Si was impressed.

"I was at Rome airport doing a sales presentation when I got the call. 'Get to Timbuktu as fast as you can' were my instructions, so here I am. Where are we going?"

"Our destination is Durham in the UK. How long will it take us to get there?"

"That's about 3,000 miles, we'd have to fly into Durham Tees Valley Airport, should take us just over five hours. We're on the same Meridian as the UK, so we should be there around ten o'clock tonight. Just need to top her up first." Captain Crowther turned and disappeared in search of fuel.

Tom had been standing within earshot. "I say Si, that plane's quite a sight. Where are we going?"

"He's going to drop us at Durham. We're off to the University. I'm afraid you'll all have to get another flight from there. Where do you live?" Si asked.

"I'm from London, Durham sounds fine. I'm sure there's an internal flight ... should be quite a ride!" Tom pulled out his mobile phone as he walked away.

Pullman and a couple of his men appeared from the airport building carrying the box. A faint frost edged the corners, an indication of the occasional use of the fire extinguisher. They walked over to the plane and pushed the box into the cargo hold just in front of the left-hand, tail mounted jet engine. Their luggage was then pushed in and packed around the box.

The re-fuelling truck disconnected and drove away. Captain Crowther walked around the plane, checking the flight surfaces and the cargo door. Satisfied, he indicated to Si he was ready and the group of civilians started to board the plane. Inside, the cabin was surprisingly roomy. The rectangular shape of the fuselage gave extra head room at the edges. The windows were like tinted glass but formed from the same fuselage material. They settled into their seats, one each side of the gangway, and strapped themselves in.

The engines whined into life and the aircraft taxied towards the start of the runway, the pitch of the engines increased to a muffled crescendo as the aircraft shot forward and was air borne almost immediately, a testimony to the light weight of the airframe. The climb away from Timbuktu was rapid as they turned to head north. The sun was setting, throwing the desert into sharp relief. and the town of Timbuktu was now just a smudge in the vast expanse of golden brown.

The pilot levelled out in the semi-darkness of the upper atmosphere, a thin blue line wrapped itself around the slight curvature of the horizon; North Africa, an enormous expanse of arid desert, unfurled beneath them.

The seat belt light went out, Si unbuckled and walked to the cockpit door and knocked.

"Come in," shouted a voice from inside.

Si stepped through the door into the small cockpit. Captain Crowther sat at the controls, a small joystick in his left hand. His co-pilot sat next to him checking their position on the digital map displayed before him.

"Hi ... we've had some incidents while we've been in Africa. I was wondering whether you could just keep on eye on the radar for me and let me know if anything unusual appears?" Si had learnt from Pullman it was better to be prepared for anything.

"Sure ... what sort of problems?" asked the co-pilot.

Si didn't want to go into detail, "some people have been trying to follow us. I'd rather they didn't know where we are."

"OK, I'll let you know if anything unusual happens."

Si thanked him and returned to his seat. Mary was gazing out of the window. He looked across at her and smiled, "let's hope we're leaving those problems behind ... I can't believe it's only three days ago I arrived in Africa!"

"A lot's happened, it's not the normal way my studies go!" laughed Mary, glad to be leaving with someone whom she felt very comfortable after her self-imposed exile.

Chapter Nineteen

Another surprise

"Contact established, over," the pilot of the F-15 reported back to base.

"Wait until they're over the sea and then destroy. It's a prototype after all, these things happen," came the reply.

"Yes sir, understood."

***

Mary and Si had been either dozing or staring out of the window, both trying to relax after the whirlwind of events during the last few days. Si watched the coast of Algiers slide under the plane from his lofty viewpoint 11 miles high, and could just pick out the coast of Spain edging the horizon. The pilot called Si over the cabin speakers.

Si stepped into the cockpit.

"Shut the door." The co-pilot looked perturbed.

"What's up?" asked Si.

"We've got a strange echo on the radar. There's a jet approaching, heading directly for our position and it doesn't have any identifying transmissions. We've tried radio contact, but there's no response."

The hairs on Si's neck started to rise. Maybe this was just a coincidence but he didn't feel like taking any chances. "How far away is it?"

"About twenty miles. At it's current speed, it should reach us in about a minute," the co-pilot estimated.

"Did you say you can become invisible to radar?" Si was starting to feel a panic rising. They were sitting ducks, completely defenceless if anyone did attack.

"Yes, we could also climb to our maximum altitude if you think we've got a problem. Not many other aircraft can get that high." suggested Crowther.

"Do it, do anything you can, I think we've got trouble." Si had noticed another smaller blip on the radar start pulling away, heading towards them.

The co-pilot had spotted it too. "Looks like a missile coming!"

The pilot flicked a few switches, pulled up the nose and pushed the throttles forward to maximum. The darkness of space filled the windshield as the plane climbed higher.

"It's still coming! This will be close!" shouted the co-pilot.

The altimeter display increased; 55,000, 56,000, .. 57,000.

The small blip on the radar started to drift from a collision course.

***

The pilot of the F-15 reported back to control, "Radar contact lost, they've disappeared! Missile's lost it's homing signal! I'm at the limit of my range, I'll have to turn back."

***

"I think we've lost it, must have been set to target using radar and it's lost our echo."

Crowther banked the plane sideways and looked out of the window to see a missile shoot underneath them followed by the unmistakable shape of an F-15.

"I used to fly those, they can't get up to this altitude ... looks like we might be OK ... who would want to destroy us?" Beads of sweet glistened on Crowther's forehead.

Si noticed the F-15 was black and unmarked. "There have been a few attempts to stop us over the last few days. I was hoping we were far enough away to be safe."

"You have upset someone! We were asked to keep this flight quiet, I'm beginning to see why."

Below them the F-15 banked round and started heading away.

"Looks like he might be operating at the edge of his range. Probably had one chance to get us, hoped we wouldn't notice until it was too late. I'm glad you suggested we monitored the radar." The pilot looked more relaxed.

Si went back into the cabin to a sea of worried faces.

"What happened?"Mary asked. "The seat belt light came on and the plane suddenly tipped back. We all thought we'd had it!"

"It's OK, they had another go at us, but they've gone now." His words didn't seem to ease the tension, only Tom seemed to have taken it in his stride.

He quietly explained to Mary what had transpired. "I'm wondering how they knew where we were heading."

Chapter Twenty

Back in the UK

"We're on approach to Durham airport, should land in about ten minutes," the pilot announced.

Si glanced across to Mary and smiled. She still looked worried. The events of the last few days made her wish she'd never cajoled him into letting her join the expedition. Then her thoughts turned to the box in the hold and the possible implications to the history of the human race. If she could confirm the find, it wouldn't do her reputation any harm either.

She wondered whether another more advanced race had populated the earth before archaeologists believed it possible. It had worried her that modern humans had populated the earth for 200,000 years and we only had evidence of any real progress; religious sites, cities, agriculture, in the last 20,000 years. She'd always wondered why it took us 180,000 years to get started!

Almost imperceptibly, the aircraft touched down onto the runway. Out of the window, she could see the airport buildings approaching. A couple of Army Ocelots sat on the tarmac. Si had contacted Pullman after the latest attack and he'd decided to send an escort to the airport to make sure they got safely to Durham University twenty-odd miles away.

The team descended the stairs and were met by a Customs Officer. He checked their passports with his portable scanner and left. Two SAS soldiers pulled the box from the cargo hold. Mary and Si grabbed their luggage, put their cases into the back of the lead Ocelot and said their goodbyes to the rest of the team.

Mary called the head of her archaeology department as they were travelling up the A1(M). Although it was approaching eleven in the evening, he was still at the University. In response to the email she had sent from Timbuktu, he had assembled a small team ready to examine the artefacts she had collected as soon as they arrived.

The internet campaign denouncing her had gathered pace and even the media were involved. Conspiracy theories were gaining strength as everyone with a view on science was joining the debate. Her boss was only too eager to try and confirm the find one way or the other. The reputation of the University was at stake. Since the debacle in 2009 about global warming, no one trusted scientists any more. After all, even the forecast calamity for the asteroid impact had not materialised.

They pulled off South Road and stopped outside the Dawson Building. The main entrance door swung open and Mary's boss, Professor Bob Cunningham, greeted them. He led the way to the laboratories in the Archaeology Department, the soldiers placed the box on a table.

"We have orders to remain outside to ensure there aren't any further problems." The soldiers left the room.

"Well Mary, what do we have?" Bob started examining the copper box. "I've never seen anything like this before, the carvings and etchings look so fresh. Let's open it up. We can put the contents in the fridge over there. Luckily, the Labs cold tonight."

Si pulled out his Swiss Army knife and slit the gaffer tape that sealed the lid. He lifted the top and they peered inside.

The tablets looked like they'd survived the journey intact. A corner was broken off the top tablet, probably from the sudden manoeuvres by the plane, but that appeared to be the only problem.

Bob lifted the fragment and examined it. Holding it up to the light, "it does look like it's been rolled from tree sap. You can see tiny fragments of debris typical of amber. Let's get the rest into the fridge, we can have a look at this piece first."

Bob walked to a microscope and positioned the sample. He crouched over and gave a gasp, "my god! ... there's a small insect in here I've never seen before. Let's get it Radiocarbon dated." He cut a small sample from the fragment, dropped it into a test tube and gave it to a researcher who hurried from the Lab towards the Carbon Dating Laboratory.

"You said you'd started to decipher the language on the tablets. Have you managed to translate anything?" Bob was starting to get excited. He couldn't believe these tablets were a fake.

"I've started to build a dictionary of words, but I haven't tried to translate any of the more complex tablets yet. We've been a bit tied up trying to save our lives!" smiled Mary.

She walked over to a laptop computer on a bench and inserted the camera card containing the images she had taken in the Library. She pulled up the tablet with the square image and explained to Bob her theory that the tablets appeared to have been created to make their translation easier.

Bob nodded as Mary pointed out the characters and their meanings. She flicked open pictures of the tablets which became increasingly more complex. Bob pointed out similarities with other ancient languages. The symbols seemed to have links to most of the known texts.

"I'm starting to see what you mean," Bob pondered. "This isn't a combination of other texts, but it could be their foundation. Each language just taking a part of the structure and evolving in a different direction. I think you're right. This could pre-date anything we've found before. It'll be interesting to see by how much when we get the dating results back."

As he spoke, the researcher hurried in with the dating sample. She went straight over to Bob, "you're not going to believe this. The sample is too old to date accurately! We're going to need a different method."

Bob turned to Mary and Si, "Radiocarbon dating doesn't work well on material more than 60,000 years old ... I wonder if there are any sand grains inside the tablets. If we can extract some, we may be able to use Optically Stimulated Luminescence dating."

Si had heard of these techniques, but needed clarification. "What will OSL do?"

"It measures the last time the sample was exposed to sunlight. You tell me the tablets have been sealed in this box and not exposed to sunlight. Should be able to test them if we can find some mineral samples in the amber." Bob turned back to the fragment under the microscope.

"What about any sand inside the box? I can't believe none got in when they were assembling the boxes. Would that work?" questioned Si.

"Good idea," said Bob, he turned to a researcher. "Check for some mineral samples in the box. See if we can get a better sample."

The researcher took a test-tube and crossed over to the box. Reaching down inside, she shook the box to gather the sand together and collected the grains, then carried it to where Bob was studying the fragment through the microscope.

He looked up and examined the test-tube. "That should be enough, take it down, let's see what we can find this time."

She rushed off, back towards the Dating Lab.

"The scientific community have been giving you a bit of a hard time," Bob commented. "Hopefully, we can get some better evidence to support your findings. I think we'll need to get back to the site to do some 'proper' archaeology. Study the structures more, burial depths, you know the sort of thing."

"Now we know where it is, we can organise a full site examination. Might need to get some funding. Do you think any of the media channels would be interested in sponsoring the dig?" asked Mary.

"Maybe ... this could be the archaeological find of the century. Quiet a scoop. I'll make a few enquiries with some media contacts." Bob went back to his microscope.

Si took Mary to one side. "You haven't mentioned Lucere and the Orbianes," he whispered.

"With the media frenzy that's going on at the moment, I don't think it will help our case if we start talking about invisible beings. Hopefully, that'll all come out when we examine the site and the texts thoroughly," Mary whispered back.

He held her arm and gave a gentle squeeze, "I've just realised, I haven't got anywhere to stay tonight. Looks like I'll be sleeping in the Lab!"

"I'm sure we can sort something out. Let's get the results from the dating and then we can go back to my place to get some sleep," winked Mary.

The researcher ran back through the door clutching a computer print-out. She rushed over to Bob. "Initial tests show a date of 101,000 years, plus or minus five percent!"

Bob stood up and smiled. He turned to Mary and Si, "looks like you're right. This is a discovery that's going to re-write human history, congratulations."

"Problem is, it's not human history. I've a few photo's I haven't shown you yet." Mary crossed over to the laptop and pulled up a new image.

Bob gasped as he realised what was on the screen. "Oh my god ... this is getting more bizarre by the minute. Where did you find these?"

Mary described the structure they had found and the strange Transcender room that contained the remains Bob was now studying.

"You're saying these tablets weren't created by our ancestors!" Bob was visibly shocked.

"From what I could tell, they're more our cousins. A bit like Neanderthal man only much more intelligent." Mary described the measurements she'd taken.

"This is going to take some careful handling. I'm not sure the world's quite ready for this yet.

We need to get our facts spot on or we'll all go down in flames. This could either make or break the University's reputation." Bob was starting to get uneasy.

"I think it's time to pack up and let this information settle overnight. We can't do much more tonight." Bob turned to his research team. "Tidy everything away, I don't want anyone talking about what's gone on here tonight. We've got to keep the lid on this for a while until we have solid scientific data. Is that understood!" Bob scanned the room making sure everyone acknowledged his instructions.

The team packed away, locked the box in the specimen room and padlocked the fridge. Then, subdued, they filed out of the building.

The SAS soldiers were still outside standing guard.

Si told them he and Mary were finished for the night and thanked them for their help. They climbed into their vehicle and disappeared.

Mary and Si started to walk back to her apartment in the University grounds. She finally had the evidence to clear her name. She linked arms and was grateful for the security she felt in his presence.

Chapter Twenty-One

Durham

Si awoke in the small hours of the morning still fully clothed. His shirt and trousers were crumpled, his shoes and socks lay where they'd dropped. Flickering lights and an eerie, orange glow illuminated the thin curtains. He got up as gently as possible so as not to disturb Mary and looked out of the window.

"Mary, Mary, quick ... come and look at this!" he shouted.

Mary struggled to come around and walked unsteadily to the window. "Oh my god, that's the Dawson Building."

Flames were erupting from the roof, visible above the tree tops, a few hundred yards away. They could hear windows shattering in the heat.

"The artefacts, all our evidence, destroyed. We've even lost the pictures ... I left the camera card in the laptop!" Mary's eyes filled.

Si dug into his pocket and pulled out a small plastic card. "Lucky I decided to take it out ... must have had a premonition! Do you think our 'friends' have paid us a visit?"

"Well, it's a bit of a coincidence ... damn! They just won't give up, will they!" she was starting to get angry.

In the distance they heard the sirens from the fire engines, blue lights bounced across the tops of the trees. They stood together at the window, arms around each other, mesmerised by the spectacle before them.

It took the Fire Brigade the rest of the night to bring the flames under control and finally stop the fire.

Mary and Si showered, dressed into fresh clothes and walked over to the burnt-out building. The roof and the internal floors had collapsed, the red brick walls looked fragile and charred; the smell of burnt wood filled the air.

Mary spotted Bob Cunningham. "Do the Fire-Brigade know what happened Bob?"

"They think it's suspicious, maybe someone with a grudge against the University, who knows?" Bob sounded weary.

Mary and Si glanced at each other.

"You don't think it's anything to do with your discovery?" Bob was starting to piece recent events together.

"I don't know," said Mary. "I can't believe anyone would want to destroy what we'd found. What can they possibly gain?"

"You do realise, if your discovery is genuine, the revelation will have major repercussions ... and not just for science. Think about the world religions. How are they going to fit this information into their belief structure?" Bob had been considering the implications all night.

"But surely the truth is what's important. Our discovery doesn't mean people can't have their faith. This challenges doctrine not faith." Mary couldn't understand hiding the truth.

"Just think, the Catholic Church for example, is one of the wealthiest organisations in the world with over a billion followers. Then, there are thirty million Muslims. They've all been taught they are the chosen people. How will that reconcile with finding a race that's superior to ours?" Bob was well aware of the pressure religions could bring to bear on science. In the past scientists had been imprisoned or even murdered for their theories.

"Do you think some religious organisation could be behind this?" Mary couldn't believe this was possible in modern society.

"Let's just say they've a lot at stake, but now it's all been destroyed, we haven't any evidence. So whoever is behind it has got their way."

"We could return to Africa and get some more evidence," said Mary defiantly. "The truth always surfaces in the end."

"I wouldn't advise that, look what's happened so far. Your lucky you're still alive, both of you," Bob was concerned.

Si had been listening with interest to the discussion. He pulled out his phone. "Hi Pullman, it's Si, how are you? ... What! ... You're joking ... ! Is anyone hurt ... ? We think they've torched the University Lab as well, everything has been destroyed! ... OK ... OK ... I'll call back later." Si thought it best to keep the information about the photographs to themselves.

Mary and Bob looked quizzically at Si

"You won't believe this, Pullman was just about to call us. There was a series of explosions in the night ... they felt the ground shake. He tracked the source down to the site. It's been completely destroyed. Even the rock outcrop with the entrance has been shattered. The sites a complete mess. It would take months of heavy machinery to get anywhere near the Library again."

Mary's eyes filled, "we've got nothing, no evidence. No one will fund an expedition with the accusations that are going around at the moment.

They've beaten us." Tears trickled down Mary's face.

"We do have one thing left," Si pulled the camera card out of his pocket. "We've still got your pictures."

Mary looked at him with sadness in her eyes. "No one will believe the pictures."

"Maybe not, but we can still translate them. Do you remember Lucere mentioned a city in Australia." Si thought back to his discussion, "perhaps we can find evidence of it's location? This time we'll keep it to ourselves."

"I think your mad if you're going to pursue this further, but you can depend on my support. As far as I'm concerned everything got destroyed in the fire. Mary, I think you need to take some leave to get over your adventures," Bob winked.

***

Sitting in his office at the university, Professor Borghese smiled as he put down the phone. At last, a call that pleased him. It seems they'd managed to destroy the evidence after all. No-one was going to take Professor Mary Freeman serious for a very long time.

Chapter Twenty-Two

Mary's Apartment

Mary and Si returned to her apartment. Opening the front door, Mary realised she hadn't even picked up her mail. She grabbed the various letters, leaflets and a small parcel. She flicked through the envelopes and finding nothing of interest, opened the parcel.

A small data stick dropped out with a note. She read the note and smiled. "I think I know what we're doing next. I'd emailed Clare, a friend of mine from college days, who worked with me for a while. She went more down the IT side. She's sent us a few programs she's written. They analyse and translate texts, thought we might find it useful."

"How does that work," asked Si.

"Seems there are three stages," said Mary reading from the note. "First we feed a scan of the text into a program, which compiles a list of all of the symbols, then we add any translations we have to the list. The second process then goes through the text, replacing any symbols that have translations. The third process looks at the result and tries to propose words that might fit in the gaps; you select some words, add them to the list and start again. Clare reckons three or four passes can give a rough translation of most languages though she's never tried it on anything as old as this. She'd like us to let her know how it goes."

"It sounds long-winded," said Si.

"Believe me, it sounds a lot quicker than working through it any other way. People have spent years translating texts like this. It took more than two years to translate Egyptian hieroglyphs after they'd found the Rosetta stone." Mary remembered.

"Let's get started." Si grabbed his laptop.

The photo's loaded, the software installed, they started processing the images. Some needed the image enhancing software before the software could recognise the symbols, but they slowly started to build a vocabulary. They worked all day, bent over the laptop, Taking it in turns to supply regular cups of tea or coffee. The intensity of the task pushed thoughts of the last few days from their minds and they started to laugh and joke about some of the words the software suggested.

Often, she would drape herself around Si's shoulders as they studied the results of the scans. She felt very comfortable and the happiest she had felt for as long as she could remember. During the afternoon, they took a rest from the screen and made love on the floor, exploring each others bodies, enjoying the intimacy of their physical contact. They took a shower together, then refreshed, they continued with the translation.

It was early evening, they'd built up a vocabulary of five or six thousand words and Mary thought it was time to try one of the later much more complex texts. Si loaded an image and set the software to work. As the results started to appear, they got more and more excited;

Great continent ... round, red rocks floating in a desert sea ... 50 circles east ... 2 circles north ... entombed within the centre of the 36 domes ... preserved for eternity ... protected by the dreamers ...

"This is going to take some working out! Do you think this might be the location of another city? A great continent with red rocks floating in a desert sea. It reminds me of Ayers Rock. Lucere said the last city was in Australia. I went there on my gap year, I was back-packing around the world visiting all of the known major meteorite impact sites. I went to a site at Henbury, the Meteorites Conservation Reserve, not far from Ayers Rock." Si could picture the massive rock which did look like it was floating in the desert of central Australia.

"These must be measurements," said Mary. "They could be references to circles. All through time, circles have been allocated 360 degrees, perhaps we need to multiply the number by 360? As for the unit, the oldest one I can think of is the Megalithic Yard, which is 0.7 metres. No-one knows where it came from, although it appears to be the unit of measurement for a very large number of separate ancient sites."

Si pulled up a picture of Australia from the internet and zoomed in on Ayers Rock. He moved the image and followed the measurements. The location he found was Kata Tjuta. Pulling up a description, it was described as rock outcrops forming thirty six domed red rocks.

"That looks like our destination. Only problem is, it's in the heart of the Uluru National Park. It's not going to be easy to get access to try and discover the hidden city. The local Aboriginals that own and manage the site are very protective." Si recalled his last visit.

"Hold on ... *protected by the dreamers* ... the Aborigines talk of their pre-history as the Dreamtime!" Mary exclaimed.

"I think we'd better start organising our holiday," Si smiled.

Chapter Twenty-Three

On vacation?

"Mary Freeman's credit card has just purchased two tickets to Sydney, Australia," the voice on the phone informed Professor Borghese. "What do you want us to do?"

"Let's hope they have decided to take a vacation ... but just in case, follow them." Borghese replaced the phone. He'd hoped this episode had ended. There had been far too much collateral damage and the Cult was getting uneasy. He couldn't afford any more mistakes.

***

Si and Mary completed their travel arrangements. They'd managed to get a late deal to fly out of Heathrow the following day. Mary packed her case and they decided to have a celebratory meal. Mary knew of an Indian Restaurant in the centre of Durham she'd been to before.

The last visit hadn't been easy, her boyfriend had chosen that moment to tell her they were finished. It also meant she'd lost her best friend. That was the night she'd decided to leave the UK and later, in the small hours, she'd found a secondment to Timbuktu. Tonight, she would have to face those demons and hopefully put the whole sorry situation behind her and clear the past so that with Si, she could look forward again.

As a precaution, before they left, Si downloaded all of the software and translation results onto a computer stick and deleted all of the history from his laptop. Armed with the stick and the camera card they left for the restaurant.

***

Some time later, a shadowy figure crept up to Mary's front door.

"You're sure ... nothing suspicious at all?" Professor Borghese was getting more confident. "The last access was flight websites? ... OK. Get yourself booked on the flight." Maybe all of the evidence had been destroyed. Perhaps Mary Freeman realised she would be unable to carry on with her work so they may as well be taking a holiday while things quietened down.

***

The restaurant was almost empty, Wednesdays weren't the busiest of days in Durham, it meant they had a choice of tables, so Mary and Si sat in a corner well away from the other diners.

For the first time since they'd met they had time to relate their life stories. Mary saw photo's of Si's two children, who were now only a few hundred miles away. Si had thought about a quick visit, but had decided against it. His ex-wife didn't like surprises and he was worried he didn't have enough time to spend with them. They were getting on with their lives and his twice yearly visits often made them unsettled.

Mary talked about her past digs around the world avoidin discussion about her past partners. She now felt they'd only been convenient relationships. She felt very different towards Si.

Over desert he reached across the table and took her hand, "you've brought me back to life. I had immersed myself into my work, shut out the world, but you've opened my eyes to new possibilities. I know we've only known each other for a few days, but I feel I've really got to know you."

Mary smiled, "we've certainly been through an awful lot. I feel like I've known you for ever."

The rest of the evening passed in a warm haze. The food was excellent and with the help of a bottle of house red, they relaxed. They laughed at each others past adventures. Mary was even starting to see the funny side of her incarceration in Gobleki Tepe.

It was late when they finally left. The evening air was balmy and stars shone from a cloudless sky. Occasionally, a gentle breeze would bring a hint of smouldering wood, reminding them of the task ahead.

Back in Mary's apartment, they snuggled under the duvet and held each other, enjoying their closeness.

***

Early next morning they braved the light drizzle and walked the one and a half miles across the city to the station to catch the train to London. Three hours later they braved the lunch-time tube from Paddington to catch the Heathrow Express.

There were a few hours to kill before they would be called for their flight; so they browsed the 'Duty Free' shops, joked over the extortionate prices and relaxed over a meal in the airport restaurant. They read the papers and Mary was pleased to discover she was no longer the main topic of the day.

They boarded the Thai Airlines super jet and settled into their seats for the twelve hour flight. They were both tired and spent most of the time trying to doze as best they could, interrupted occasionally by the stewardess offering them refreshments and in-flight meals.

Bangkok, their stop-over, was hot. The connecting flight was the following day, so they'd decided to spend the time sightseeing. They hailed a taxi outside the airport and made their way to their hotel to unpack a few things before exploring the city.

Reflected in a shop, Si noticed someone standing on the other side of the street watching them. He recognised the man and realised he had been on their train from Durham and on their flight. It was too much of a coincidence. He turned to Mary and whispered, "Don't look now but there's a man on the other side of the street ... just look at the reflection in the window ..."

"The guy in the dark jacket?" said Mary.

"... that's him, I think he's following us. Let's go in this shop and see if he's still there when we come out," suggested Si.

They went into the shop and browsed the various shelves full of tourist trinkets. Si kept glancing out of the window. The man leaned against a post, trying to look unobtrusive as shoppers passed by.

"Let's go back down the street the way we came to see if he follows." Si was trying to work out how you loose a tail, something he'd not had to do before.

They walked back down the street, trying to look as casual as possible. The man strolled after them, looking in shop windows. Si spotted a small bar and went in followed by Mary. In the dark interior, the waiter greeted them, palms together and with a gentle bow of his head, in the traditional Thai manner.

Si asked for a table near the window. They settled down and browsed the menu, watching the man take up a position opposite, leaning against a wall. The waiter came and took their order for drinks.

Si asked the waiter for the toilet and disappeared towards the back of the Bar. Five minutes later he returned, "I think I've got an idea. At the back is another small bar looking out onto a side street, I think it's mainly for locals. When we've finished, we'll leave through the back. That way we might shake him off."

Mary looked across the street to the man, still leaning against the wall, reading a magazine. "But they'll know where we're staying, he'll only have to go back to the Hotel and wait for us."

"True, but it gives us some time to think." They finished their drinks, Mary went first, Si paid the bill and joined her in the back street. They headed down the alley, meandered around scooters and overflowing rubbish bins, ducked under laundry which hung from house to house.

Finally, they came out into a square opposite the Wat Traimit shrine. They decided to go inside to view the golden Buddha, probably the largest in the world. Famous for being pasted over with stucco to fool the looting Burmese army.

When they came out of the shrine, Si glanced across the square to see the man sitting on a bench on the opposite side. "He's over there. How on earth did he find us!"

"Remember what Pullman said about mobile phones, they can track anybody anywhere if the phones switched on. They must be tracking us." She felt very uneasy.

"You're right! Let's see if we can loose him again ... I've got an idea."

Si went back into the shrine and she followed. While inside, he had noticed a door at the back. They passed around a group of tourists listening to a local guide and slipped out of the door. Once outside, he saw a group of children playing football in a side street. He asked Mary to delete her phone book and messages and did the same with his own.

He then took the two phones and walked over to the boys. "Do you speak English, he said to the oldest boy."

He nodded.

"Would you like a phone?" Si asked.

He nodded.

Si offered him the two phones.

"Why?" asked the boy not trusting the offer.

"We don't need them any more, thought you might like them."

The boy took them with a grin and ran back to his friends, showing them his prize. He tucked the ball under his arm and ran down the street.

"Hopefully, that will keep our friend busy and give us time to sort something out." Si had got a plan. "Now, we need to find the offices of Thai Airlines."

"Why do need to go there?" Mary was confused.

"Because we're going to change our flight booking." Si looked around for some form of transport. He saw the sign to Hualamphong Station. "We should be able to get a taxi there," he said pointing at the sign. They walked the short distance, constantly looking behind them to ensure they weren't being followed.

***

At first, the taxi driver wasn't keen to take the journey. When they arrived, they realised why; the airline ticket office was only round the corner, a five minute walk away, in Silom Road. Si paid the fare and gave him a generous tip, which brought a smile back to his face.

They entered the offices and Si explained they wanted to change their flight to Australia. He noticed they also flew to Perth in Western Australia.

"That would put them completely off the scent," Si whispered to Mary.

The clerk processed their request and said there was nothing further to pay. Perth was closer than Sydney, so the difference in fare paid for the booking amendment. The next available flight was that evening at ten o'clock. Si and Mary thanked the clerk and left. They managed to catch a taxi back to their hotel, grabbed their bags and got back in the waiting taxi. They'd decided to head straight back to the airport before their tail realised they'd given him the slip and he then headed back to the hotel. Luckily, the Hotel bill had been pre-paid so they didn't need to check out.

***

"They've given me the slip, must have realised we were watching them. Just found their phones. They'd given them to some kids who sold them to a second-hand dealer." He was not happy to have been fooled so easily.

"Get back to their hotel and keep a watch. Find out if they've checked out. Let me know as soon as you find out." Borghese wasn't pleased, his operatives' incompetence had alerted them. It was going to be more difficult to keep track.

***

Mary and Si boarded the plane and settled down for another long flight. This time the subject of the conversation changed to their mysterious opponents.

"They appear to be very well connected, lots of resources at their disposal, men able to follow us half way across the world, access to phone tracking, who are they and what do they want?" Si shook his head in disbelief.

"Why would anyone want to hide what could be the archaeological find of the century?" Mary was equally amazed.

"Perhaps that's the key. What is the real impact of this find?" asked Si.

"Well, it'll upset quiet a few archaeologists, that's for sure, rewrite human history, update our branch of the evolutionary tree, cause a rethink for theologians ... "

"Hold it there, I can't imagine a few scientists being upset about being wrong, it happens all the time with new discoveries and history is always being re-written. But the Churches, they may have a lot to lose. As Bob had said, this find will mean man wasn't necessarily at the pinnacle of evolution. Sure, we've survived, but at what cost to the environment? In many ways, the Orbianes were still more advanced than we are now. The Churches are multi-million pound businesses. That could all be in jeopardy, they've suppressed things before, even massacred millions of people in the name of religion. Are they somehow behind all this?" Si didn't like the way his thoughts were develping.

"There's always been a conflict between the Churches and science. Many leading scientists of their day have been locked up or murdered for their 'heretic' ideas in the past. Do you think it's still going on?" Now Mary was getting uncomfortable.

"All I do know is we're going to have to be extra careful. I wish we had more support. I certainly miss Pullman at times like this," smiled Si.

"He did look after us, didn't he, perhaps we should give him a call when we land." Mary smiled too.

They reclined their seats, settled down, held hands under the flight blankets and dozed.

Chapter Twenty-Four

Perth, Australia

They arrived in Perth early in the morning. By the time they'd collected their cases and passed through Customs, the sun had risen to start a new day.

They made their way to one of the bank outlets in the main terminal hall.

"I'm going to draw out as much money as I can. They can probably track any transactions we do, so they'll know we've been here, but if we use cash we can then put them off the scent." Si had been thinking about this since they left Bangkok.

"I'll draw out what I can as well. We've still got quite a way to go and I think it's going to be expensive!" Mary pulled out her cards.

They left the Bank with a large bag full of Australian dollars and caught a taxi to the centre of Perth. They searched around for an airline who could book them a flight to Ayers Rock. A Quantas flight left at ten o'clock that morning, arriving at Ayers Rock just after midday.

They'd got time to spare at the airport so they caught the shuttle bus from Terminal 1 to Terminal 3, the domestic flights terminal and made their way to the Hudsons Coffee outlet. While they'd dozed on the flight, they'd missed their in-flight meal and now realised they were hungry.

Si kept scanning the part of the airport concourse that was visible to him, checking for any sign of anyone following them. One suspicious man who seemed to be hanging around finally met what looked like his daughter and they disappeared towards the exit laughing.

Their flight was called and they made their way to the Gate. Settled into couple of seats near the front of the aircraft, where Si could watch the other passengers boarding. No-one aroused his suspicions, maybe they'd finally shaken off any tail.

Mary spotted their destination out of the aircraft window as the massive red rock rose from the barren earth. It was visible for miles. It wasn't surprising this should feature so strongly in Aboriginal folk lore.

They landed at Connellan Airport and after collecting their bags, they hired a Toyota and headed down Coote Road for the Lasetter Highway and the town of Yulara.

In Yulara, they discovered that the Ayers Rock area, properly known by the Aboriginal name of Uluru, was managed by an Aboriginal community based in Mutitjulu. Mary and Si realised, if they wanted to explore the area freely in order to find the lost city, then they would need permission from it's Aboriginal owners.

They decided to drive the twenty eight kilometres to Mutitjulu to try and talk to the community leaders.

***

"They didn't board the flight to Sydney. I've lost them ... !" said the voice on the phone.

"They're in Perth ... their credit cards have been used at the Airport. I'm afraid they knew you were tailing them. Get a flight to Perth. Try and find out where they've gone." Annoyed, Borghese replaced the handset.

***

Si parked the car near the visitor centre at Mutitjulu and they wandered in. Sitting in the corner behind a counter was an Aboriginal woman weaving a basket from dried grasses. A colourful cotton dress covered her ample proportions.

"Hi, how long have the Aboriginal people lived here?" asked Si.

"We have occupied these lands for all time. Aboriginal people believe in the beginning there was a time known as *Tjukurpa* 'the Dreamtime'. When back in the distant past the creator ancestors, known as the First Peoples, travelled across the land. We are their direct descendants and are tasked with protecting the land and their traditions."

Mary asked, "these First people, what do your stories say of them?"

"They were bearers of great knowledge, passing on wisdom and skills. They built great cities and cared for all things. Their time passed and we have accepted responsibility to maintain memories until knowledge is understood again." Boggabri turned to a customer who was purchasing a copy of an Aboriginal cave painting.

Si waited for the customer to leave. "Is it possible to visit Kata Tjuta?"

" Kata Tjuta is very sacred to my people. We restrict access. Why would you visit there?" asked Boggabri.

"I'm Si and this is Mary, we believe there's something important there from the Dreamtime. We have information that indicates there may be a lost city," Si explained hoping he wasn't disclosing too much.

Boggabri looked deep into his eyes. Si thought he had gone too far and Mary fidgeted uneasily with some Ayers Rock key-rings on the counter. A difficult minute passed.

"My name is Boggabri, which means Rain Bird. I'm member of Council of Elders who manage access to sites. You should ask council in person. Are you willing to do that?"

"Yes, I'd be happy too," Si felt they'd made a breakthrough. He was glad he had trusted his instincts.

"We have meeting at four o'clock this afternoon in Community Hall next door. Can you be there?" she asked.

"Yes, we'll be there. Thank you." Si was getting quite excited at the prospect of meeting the council, although he had no idea what he was going to say.

Chapter Twenty-Five

Mutitjulu

When the time arrived, they made their way to the Community Centre and entered the single story building. In a room off to the right, they could hear subdued conversation. Mary and Si entered to find eight Aboriginal people sitting in a semi-circle in the middle of the room. They recognised Boggabri, who signalled for them to come in and sit in two chairs that had been placed opposite.

One of the Council members, wearing a bright short sleeved shirt and brown shorts, got up and closed the door. His weathered skin sat in comfortable folds around his broad flattened nose. A white curly beard hid his chin. An impish smile flashed across his face as he returned to his chair. He leaned forward and introduced himself. "I'm Wundurra head of Council. Boggabri tells me you wish to visit one of our sacred sites. Can I ask why?"

Si looked at Mary, "I think we should tell them everything ... we've got nothing to lose."

She nodded. Mary started to tell the story from the beginning, the asteroid impact, the Library and even the attempts to obliterate the site. As she talked, the Council members glanced at each other, nodding occasionally, making the odd comment in their native language.

When she had finished, Wundurra spoke to the council. They looked at Mary and Si and then back to Wundurra, nods ended the discussion.

"In our dream stories, it is predicted strangers will come who seek knowledge of First People. The stories say these people will already have knowledge and they must pass a test. Will you do test?" asked Wundurra.

"What is the test?" Mary was a bit uncomfortable about accepting the challenge without knowing what it was.

"We have ancient text, written by 'First People'. If you can read it, you are people talked of in dreams."

"I'll certainly have a try," responded Mary.

One of the council members walked over to a wooden box in the corner of the room, opened the lid, took out a wooden tablet and placed it on the table next to the box.

Mary walked nervously over to the table, then for a moment she studied the text carved into the tablet, turned to Si and smiled. "This is the same writing from the Library," the excitement in her voice difficult to conceal. "Pass me the lap-top and the data stick."

Si had been nursing the computer on his lap. He walked over, switched on and waited impatiently for the operating system to power up. He pulled the data stick from his pocket and inserted it into the computer. Mary called up the vocabulary they had built and started to write down her translation of the text. A look of amazement slowly spread across her face.

After about ten minutes of careful study and re-checking, Mary straightened, "I think I can tell you what it says."

It is time for the knowledge
of the Orbianes to be passed
to our friends.
Use it wisely.

The council members looked at each other in disbelief. Boggabri was the first to speak. "I saw in their eyes, their souls were true."

Wundurra nodded, "their auras are clear. Our task to protect writings is at an end." He turned to Mary and Si. "The teachings tell us to help you in any way to pass knowledge to world. What do you wish us to do?"

"Can you lead us to the ancient knowledge?" asked Mary.

"Yes, we keep the location secret and ensure no one goes to the area. It will be dusk soon. I propose we take you to sacred place tomorrow. We will meet here at seven o'clock tomorrow morning," smiled Wundurra.

"There is just one thing. We told you of the people trying to destroy the knowledge. They're very resourceful. We've tried to keep our destination secret but they seem to have eyes and ears everywhere. Can we ask that you stay vigilant and should anyone or anything appear unusual, let us know." Si didn't want to underestimate their opponents again.

"The story also tells of false prophet who will try to keep knowledge secret. We will look out for him. We are tasked by ancient stories to ensure your protection. We will not fail." Wundurra's name didn't mean 'Warrior' without reason.

Chapter Twenty-Six

Kata Tjuta

Mary and Si were given a room in Boggabri's house as there were no hotels in Mutitjulu. They sat on the wooden porch watching the breathtaking display of constantly changing colours on Ayers Rock as the sun went down.

Boggabri chatted about the history behind the Uluru National Park and the way the Australian Government had gone back on part of their agreement, when handing ownership and control back to the Aboriginal People, the Anangu. Something the Government subsequently set straight. It was now nearly half way through the 99 year lease. In just over fifty years, the Anangu would have total ownership of their sacred places.

Mary and Si went to bed full of stories about the 'First People'. It seemed the Aboriginal people were the only race left on earth who can be traced back to the time of the Orbianes. Some archaeologists believe Aboriginal people may have come to Australia 125,000 years ago.

***

Seven o'clock, they were waiting outside the Community Centre as the Australian sun started to climb.

A battered Toyota Land Cruiser pulled up on the car park and Wundurra climbed out. "I had dream last night First People were slowly dissolving into light. They flew around Uluru and Kata Tjuta like stars leaving patterns in night sky.

I feel it's good omen but there was a dark cloud in distance, so we must stay vigilant."

Mary and Si nodded and climbed into the 4x4. Wundurra knocked it into gear and accelerated away. They bounced down the red dust road skirting close to the southern most end of Ayers Rock and joined the Uluru Road, until it rejoined the Lasetter Highway.

"The entrance to city has been lost. Only Council members are aware of symbols that may help find it," Wundurra explained.

"So, you haven't seen inside yourself?" queried Mary.

In the distance, the red stone mounds of Kata Tjuta rose from the barren land. Mount Olga, the highest, at just over one thousand metres above sea level, was some two hundred metres higher than Ayers Rock.

"No, we can only open entrance when people in stories have arrived; only they will know how to open door." Wundurra looked at them, "there are symbols to interpret when we get to the place."

They branched right onto another red dirt road that cut through flat featureless bush with occasional patches of low lying shrub. Wundurra drove with surprising skill considering his age. The road swung around the south side of Kata Tjuta and ahead was a car park.

"So you can't read the First People's writing?" asked Mary.

"No, we have been told meaning of tablet through story. That is how we know what is written." Wundurra parked the vehicle, grabbed his back-pack and climbed down.

The three stood and looked up in awe at the massive red mounds silhouetted against the bright morning sky. "Symbols are high up in gulley. It's a climb!" Wundurra warned.

They took the tourist footpath, worn down by thousands of feet, and headed for a gap between two red mounds. As they crested the rise, Wundurra turned right off the path and started to climb the red stone slope.

After a while they found themselves underneath an overhanging fold of rock that cut across the side of the hill. They were completely hidden from anyone. The cool shade was very welcome, the climb had been more exhausting than they'd expected. Wundurra strode forward, seemingly unaffected by the exertion for all his seventy years. Mary and Si panted behind.

"Not far, just at crest of gulley," he pointed up the slope.

They rested for a few minutes and then started out again. At the crest, Wundurra stopped. He stared at the rock face. A few bushes were clinging precariously to life on the barren dry rock. Wundurra pushed behind them and bent down.

"These are symbols." He pointed to some carvings hidden behind the bushes and protected by the overhanging rock above.

Mary and Si looked at each other. They couldn't see any feature, except the carvings. No cave, no crevice, nothing that suggested an entrance to a lost city.

Mary copied the carvings onto her notepad, carefully identifying every feature. "The writing is quite weathered. Might have to make a guess at some of the symbols."

She took the laptop from Si and settled down on a convenient rock in the shade and started to decipher the text.

Wundurra and Si watched and waited.

After some scribbling and crossing out, Mary felt she had a grasp of the meaning. "I've had to make a few guesses where it's worn, but I think it says,

Behind you and high overhead,
a stone lies flat shaped like a bed.
Near another the place is under,
Knowledge to crack the world asunder.

I've had to improvise a few words, but I think that's what's written."

The three turned and gazed up at the rock face.

"It's too steep. We go back down gulley. There's a slope we can use to reach top." Wundurra turned and started back down the slope.

"What do you think that last line means?" Si asked Mary as they picked their way over the loose stones.

"I'm not sure, but I think they're trying to warn us to use the knowledge wisely. After all, for all their knowledge, their civilisation collapsed just like all other major civilisations."

They returned to the beginning of the gulley. Wundurra turned and started to climb the red stone slope towards the summit. As they went higher, the view opened out and the great expanse of bush spread to the horizon. In the distance, Ayers Rock rose from the ground, as if floating on a red sea.

At the top of the mound they found a large flat stone with a few smaller ones scattered around.

"The large one could be the bed, which means one of these other stones near might be the entrance ... they don't look very promising," said Si glancing around.

Wundurra started digging with his hand under a circular slab about two metres in diameter.

"Others have been eroded from rock, this stone is at different angle to stone beneath, as if it's been placed here." Wundurra continued to clear the debris from around the base. "It seems bottom has been shaped, there are bulges underneath, almost like feet ... OK that's enough. Help me push it."

Mary and Si leaned against the slab of rock with Wundurra and pushed hard. Nothing happened. They got a better purchase and pushed with all their might. The stone appeared to move a fraction.

"We need something to help, I've got ropes and pulleys in car." Wundurra turned to go.

"Do you need a hand to carry anything?" asked Si.

"You wait here. Save your energy for when we get inside," he smiled.

Chapter Twenty-Seven

The lost city

Mary and Si spent their time waiting for Wundurra by speculating about what they might find beneath the slab. Would there be an entrance? Would the city be similar to the Sahara site? Would the knowledge be stored in the same way? Lot's of questions, but no answers until they could move the slab.

Wundurra returned after half an hour carrying a coil of rope and swinging a couple of pulley blocks. He lashed the pulleys to the larger slab, then threw the rope around the circular stone. They started to pull. Slowly, inch by inch, the stone started to move, grinding across the red stone surface. After it had moved a few feet they stopped to rest. Si walked over and looked at what had been exposed. The edge of a hole was visible, disappearing down into the rock.

"We need to move it the same distance again," called Si, "there's a shaft underneath."

They grabbed the ropes again with renewed energy ignoring the hot Australian sun burning down above them. The stone continued to edge it's way across the opening. By the time it was clear, all three were soaked in sweat. They sat on the edge of the slab and recovered their breath as they looked down into the shaft.

"There appear to be footholds cut into the sides. I wonder how far down it goes?" Si pondered.

Wundurra picked up a small rock and dropped it into the hole, which made a faint crash only a second later.

"About ten metres ... quite a climb down. I'll go first and check out what's at the bottom," volunteered Si. He swung his legs over the hole, found his footing and started to clamber down, bracing himself against the side of the shaft. Wundurra pulled a torch out of his bag and shone it into the darkness for Si to pick out the footholds.

Si reached the bottom and caught the torch dropped by Wundurra. As he looked around, he realised he was standing in a short tunnel lit at the far end. He walked down and emerged onto a ledge overlooking a large chamber, like the dome of a Cathedral. In the centre of the dome, a huge crystal hung from the ceiling, illuminating the cavern and the floor far below. To his side, steps cut into the rock descended across the face of the dome.

He called up to the others to come down. Mary passed the laptop to Wundurra, who put it in his rucksack. Then she started to climb down, picking her way with care, unsure about the darkness below. Si stood at the bottom shining the torch and ready to break her fall should the rock give way. Wundurra followed.

"We knew from stories of Dreamtime these rocks were special." Wundurra looked around in amazement from their vantage point on the ledge. "Our stories talk of First People rising out of stone. We never thought they were living inside ... where is light coming from?"

"My guess is the crystals are somehow connected to the outside and are concentrating the sun's rays inside the caves. I expect the crystals in the Sahara would have worked, but they were buried under sand which blocked the sunlight." Si started to descend the steps, checking as he went that they were safe.

The steps clung to the side of the hundred metre diameter dome in a great sweep. They eventually reached the base almost directly underneath where they had started. The floor was clear except for a raised circular platform in the centre about three metres in diameter and one metre above the floor. It appeared as if this was once some great gathering space.

Engraved around the edge of the platform were symbols.

"These are Orbiane," said Mary. She pulled open the laptop and checked the symbols. "*Respect for our world, freedom of choice, equality for all, individual responsibility.*" She walked around translating the symbols.

Si scanned the walls looking for a doorway or some other exit. Immediately opposite he spotted two large doors. "That looks like the way out," he pointed.

They walked over. The doors were a similar construction to the ones they had seen in Africa. Si found a lever and pressed down, the lever creaked and the doors started to open. They stepped through and heard a rustling noise.

Wundurra located the source of the sound, "Hold it ... there ... it's snake." As he spoke, a brick-red snake slithered out of sight. "They're dangerous, should leave us alone, but don't corner one. There's probably a few here, found their way in, using it as breeding ground."

"How dangerous are they?" Mary didn't like snakes at all.

They're Minggamin, you call them Desert Death Adder. If you get bitten, we've got 50/50 chance of getting you back for anti-serum before you go into coma. So, watch were you put your hands and feet!" Wundurra checked the rest of the floor as he spoke.

Si scanned the room which looked like some sort of processional way. It was about five metres wide with a domed roof, smaller crystals emitted a gentle glow at intervals down the arched roof. In alcoves at intervals along each wall, were carved statues. Some he recognised as Orbiane, tall and slender like the remains they'd found in the Transcender room, but they were mixed in with human statues.

Wundurra stared at the statues, "these are like the people in cave paintings I've seen!"

Mary looked at the symbols on the base of each statue, " *.......... Healer, ... Builder, ... Thinker, ... Well Maker,"* she translated, "the first word must be their names, but I haven't got those words in the vocabulary. Seems like they revered people's skills. It's interesting there are human statues as well, they seem to be associated to more physical tasks. Remember Lucere saying the humans helped them with more physical activities."

Wundurra went up to the Well Maker, a snake slid behind out of sight. "Looks like mix between you and I, not European, not Aboriginal. Stamp your feet as you walk, warns snakes were coming and hopefully, they'll disappear."

Si smiled at Mary who put extra effort into stamping her feet as they walked the arched way.

After about two hundred metres it opened out into a large square, but this time they could pick out many tiers cut into the walls with arched openings and stone steps. Again, a large crystal in the centre of the roof bathed the square in light.

"Just think, this place may have been lighting up for who knows how many centuries and no one knew it was here!" Si walked over to the first opening and peered in. A high room about four metres square, ledges cut into the walls, with a small version of the crystal hanging from the roof. Cut into the far wall was another archway. He walked through to find a second room of roughly the same size, a stone ledge down each side with a stone plinth three metres by two metres in the centre. He jumped as a snake slithered past him, surprised by his entrance.

"This must be one of their living spaces. This front room could be the living area and the back room could be the sleeping area." said Mary, who had followed him.

As they came out they found Wundurra wandering around with his eyes wide in amazement. "I can't believe we have been protecting such incredible place. I found washing area, basins cut into wall, channels in floor to take away water. Water source must have dried up ... there are more walkways which seem to go in all directions. This place must be huge!"

"It's also ghostly, there's no sign of habitation, no tools, or utensils, it's as if it's been completely cleaned out." Mary couldn't fit the pieces together, an advanced civilisation, but no evidence of their existence, except for the caves themselves.

"We need to find the library ... if it exists. None of this is firm evidence. This place is like a maze

... where do you think the library might be?" Mary was concerned that it was impossible to date stone structures. She needed something more tangible to recover her reputation.

"This place took some creating, so I'd guess there's some sort of plan. The pathway we came down looked important, perhaps the next significant route would be on the opposite side?" wondered Si.

They looked across, an archway rose towards the roof. "That could be the way," said Mary, "let's go."

As they crossed the square, Si noticed a circular ring of stone in the middle. He leaned over and looked down the deep shaft in it's centre. The hole was edged black, he rubbed it with his finger and sniffed. *Charcoal* he thought to himself.

Mary and Wundurra had reached the arch.

"It looks like a major pathway ... come on Si," called Mary.

Si joined them and they walked down to another large square chamber. There were more dwellings covering the walls with steps and ledges to entrances higher up. Mary estimated there must be around one hundred entrances in each of the last two squares they'd seen.

Si spotted something. He walked over to find a large stone sphere mounted on a stone pillar in the middle of the square. Above it hung an enormous crystal. As he got closer he could see carvings on the surface of the sphere. He realised it was a globe of the earth with continents etched into it's surface. He walked around and checked the details. It was a fairly accurate representation of the world today, although there were more land masses shown with unknown lands in the Pacific and the Atlantic oceans. Si realised this would be true if the ocean levels were lower than they were today. Even Antarctica was shown, something that hadn't been officially discovered until the 1820's.

Mary started to translate the symbols carved around the base. "*Study and learn. Our Mother and Father who feeds and protects us. This is the responsibility of us all.*"

"This must be where we learnt our beliefs. We have same responsibilities in our culture." Wundurra was starting to understand how his history was so intertwined with the mysterious people who had built this city.

Mary looked around the square and noticed a pillared doorway on the right-hand side, with two large doors. As she walked over, she translated the symbols above the door. "*Knowledge* ... this must be it, their library."

Chapter Twenty-Eight

Another Library

As they approached the imposing doors, Si hoped they wouldn't have to open them in the same way as before. Not much chance of any direct sunlight buried inside this rock! He examined the doors but couldn't find any obvious opening mechanism.

Mary also examined the doorway for any clues. Written across the lintel were more symbols. She opened the lap-top and translated, "*A turn of the earth will expose our knowledge* ... What does that mean, do we have to wait a day? Maybe they open when it's dark? What do you think?"

Si looked back at the huge globe at the centre of the square. "Perhaps it's something to do with that?"

He walked back and started to examine the object. He noticed hand-sized indentations around the centre. One in the middle of the Sahara, one at the top of South America, one in the centre of Australia and one in China. "You don't think it turns, do you?" He stood on the base and grasped one of the hand-holds. He tried to turn the globe but nothing happened.

Wundurra rushed over and stood on the opposite side. "Do you know which way?"

"I'd expect it'll turn the way the earth rotates, towards the east .. let's try that first," said Si pushing with all his strength. Wundurra did the same on the other side.

Slowly, very slowly, the globe turned. "A full turn," called Si.

The two men struggled around the base dragging the globe with them. As they returned to their starting positions, Mary shouted from the doorway, "It's opening ... well done!"

They walked into the library. A crystal from the ceiling lit the room showing the now familiar tiers of shelves lined with copper boxes. But in the centre of the room on a raised slab sat an Orbiane. Wundurra's jaw dropped and he fell to his knees, Mary gasped and Si froze. They stood there for what seemed like minutes, wondering whether this was a statue or a Mummy. They realised as the Orbiane turned his head, he was alive!

"Welcome," he spoke in a deep sonorous voice Si immediately recognised.

"Lucere, is it you?" Si blurted out.

"*Yes, it is I. I thought with all you have learned, you are ready to see my true form.*"

Lucere's mouth didn't move, but Si was hearing the voice inside his head. He looked at the others and realised they could hear as well.

"The stories are true ... the cave paintings," Wundurra could hardly speak as he held back his emotions, "after all these centuries, our beliefs were true."

"*Indeed, your people have done well to protect our knowledge for so long. We knew we could trust you. You should be very proud.*"

"Why have you returned?" asked Mary.

"*We feel your journey is almost at an end and we wanted to thank you for your tenacity and also to help you understand the end of our civilisation.*"

"I have so many questions, so many things I don't understand," then Mary had an idea.

"Lucere, can I record our conversation?" She remembered there was a web cam on her laptop.

"*You may ... anything that will help you understand.*"

Mary set the laptop down with the screen facing Lucere, opened up the software and checked she'd got everything lined up. Lucere's image appeared on the screen.

He stood up, "*Come, sit down.*" His long thin arm waved gracefully at the stone ledges.

They sat down and looked up. He was at least eight feet tall, long slender legs a thin torso and a large triangular shaped head, the chin being much narrower than the broad skull. His large eyes flashed with light, just as they had in Timbuktu.

"*There is so much to tell you. Everything is contained in these chests, but it will no doubt take you many years to translate. We felt you should know the important parts of our history. It will help you with the last part of your task.*"

"What do you mean, the last part of our task?" Mary was hoping that finding the Library was the end of their search.

"*Soon, someone will come to dissuade you from disclosing this knowledge. What happens next will be your decision. Only you can judge the impact this revelation will have on your society.*"

"Is this the false prophet talked about in stories?" asked Wundurra, composing himself.

"*Indeed it is. You have carried these stories through the generations with surprising accuracy. It is important you listen to what he has to say. He has valid concerns you must balance against your own ideals. Only then can a fair decision be made based on truth.*"

"How will this Prophet know where we are?" asked Si.

"*You must make your presence known. I'm sure you know how that can be done. Now, let me tell you our history.*"

Chapter Twenty-Nine

A history lesson

"Our ancestors first evolved more than two hundred thousand orbits ago alongside your ancestors. You humans concentrated on living within the limits of nature, sharing the land with the other creatures. We had a much more developed brain and started to develop tools and methods that allowed us to manipulate our environment.

Over many years, our civilisation allowed us to become more intellectual, perfecting our science and our language. Eventually we developed cities all around the world. We even constructed large images across the earth directed from aerial platforms supported by warm air. We felt we were the masters of our destiny."

"What sort of things are you talking about?" queried Si.

"Do you mean the Easter Island figures, the Olmec heads, the Pyramids, Stonehenge, the giant markings in Nazca, South America which now look like Orbiane symbols, possibly even Atlantis," asked Mary. "Oh, the list could be endless. All things about which we are unsure of their origins."

"That's correct, but during this period, we became physically weaker, not requiring strength for our advanced style of living. We started to encourage a link between your society and ours. Up to that point we had lived quite separately. You wandered the earth in small groups while we concentrated our people into cities.

We needed your physical abilities help to maintain our society. In return we showed you how to develop metal tools, build stone structures, control water for irrigation, grow your own food."

"Are you saying all of the breakthroughs made by man were actually driven by your society?" asked Mary. "That would explain why so many things suddenly appeared in our history with no evidence of their evolution."

"The relationship between our societies was mutually beneficial. You preferred your life-style, helping us when we needed it and we continued our life-style, developing new ideas. We didn't realise we were journeying down a dead end. Changes were happening in the world that were going to destroy us."

"What sort of changes?" asked Si.

"First came the ice time. Great sheets of ice suffocated many of our cities. Our people migrated to warmer areas around the equator, but these were arduous journeys for us. We didn't have the stamina and many died in the process. Then, tens of thousands of years later, the ice melted and many of our new cities were drowned as the sea levels rose, flooding enormous areas of land, sometimes without warning. Our population had started to recover but these events just wiped out any progress we had made. We were now restricted to a few centres around the world. You have now been to two, another in Ecuador was found, but destroyed."

"A friend of mine was killed in that forest fire," said Mary with anger in her eyes. Si reached out and held her hand.

"The cities we created worked with heat from the centre of the earth and light from the sun. As

the earth evolved, this city lost it's heat energy and it's water supply. The Orbianes realised the world was changing so they left on a journey north to where you call Darwin, over 1,000 miles away. They wanted to find the Saharan city because they knew about the preparations there for conversion to light beings. They knew they might not survive the journey but they didn't feel they had any choice. Our human friends joined them on the journey to Darwin and they helped us to live off the land."

"How did they travel, did they walk?" asked Si.

"They walked, it took much time, but the ground was so difficult many died on the journey. When they got to the coast where they had first come to Australia, they found the floods from the ice melt had flooded the land bridge and cut off Australia. They didn't have resources to build boats so they settled for a while on the coast and waited to die. The humans made paintings of us in the caves, to preserve our memory."

"I've seen Cave Art, tall thin people. We thought it was just style ... but it was paintings of Orbianes." Wundurra was mesmerised, he had been to the famous caves near Darwin.

Lucere looked at Wundurra. *"When the last Orbiane who embarked on the journey died, you're people took on the responsibility to protect our secrets just as you had cared for us in life. That was the end of your Dreamtime and the start of your population of Australia."*

"I believe Aboriginal people are oldest continuous civilisation on earth. We have no written history, everything was passed down as stories and pictures. Perhaps ancestors knew it was written by Orbianes and didn't see the need to write our stories." Wundurra was now even more proud of his heritage.

Mary was still trying to grasp the enormity of the discovery. "We need to get this story to the world. This will re-write human history and help us to answer so many of the unanswered questions in our pre-history."

"I believe I have passed on enough knowledge for you to finish the task you have undertaken. I trust you will make the right decisions." Lucere's image faded, coalesced into a bright light and disappeared through the roof.

Wundurra looked at Mary and Si with eyes wide in amazement. "I can't believe what I've just experienced. I can now see why you were so determined to find this place."

Si looked at his watch and realised they had been inside the caverns for four hours. "What time's sunset here?"

"Not long now, we go back to Mutitjulu. I must report to council. There is much to consider." Wundurra turned to go.

"We will return won't we?" asked Mary, worried Wundurra might prevent them from coming back.

"You have revealed part of our history. We respect your wishes, I need to know how council want to deal with these events."

Chapter Thirty

A council decision

They arrived back at Mutitjulu as dusk fell, the sun lighting Ayers Rock a deep red. Wundurra stopped at Boggabri's house and told her about the council meeting.

She was just starting to prepare a meal of Kangaroo and Yam. She turned to Mary and Si "I've got to attend meeting, food will be ready about eight, is that OK?"

"That's fine, it'll give us time to wash off the red dust of the outback," said Mary.

Boggabri left for the meeting. Mary and Si stripped off ready for a shower. Si threw himself onto the bed and said, "you shower first."

Mary looked at his slim athletic body and couldn't resist jumping on top. She gave him a passionate kiss, her hair cascading over his face and felt him respond. "Maybe the shower can wait!"

Their discoveries had charged them with adrenalin and their love making was full of energy.

After their showers, they discussed the events of the day. Mary felt elated she could now clear her name.

"What about the Torah Cult?" asked Si. "Wundurra mentioned the 'false prophet' in their story. Isn't it time we made contact. I can't see them trying to destroy this site!"

"They seem to be able to latch onto our emails, perhaps it's time to give them a nudge." Mary thought about Bob Cunningham and the fire. "I'm going to send Bob an email to tell him what we've discovered. It might help him to know we haven't lost everything and the Torah Cult might make a move."

"Good idea," agreed Si. "I wonder if there's Internet access here?"

"I'll ask Boggabri when she gets back."

***

When Boggabri returned, she told them the council would like to discuss their discovery at a meeting in the morning. She then finished preparations for the meal as Mary and Si headed for the Community Centre to use the Internet computer.

"This should be a nice email to wake up to," commented Mary as she typed the main points of the day.

***

As expected, an Internet worm detected Mary's email address and sent a copy of the email to an extra Inbox.

The computer screen in Professor Borghese's office displayed an incoming message. He studied it carefully and sat back in his chair, fingertips together, deep in thought.

This time it wasn't possible to hide the evidence, the site is much too public. Denigrating Mary's reputation wouldn't keep the evidence suppressed for long. There's one last course of action he could take. It would be risky and would expose the Torah Cult, but it was the only avenue left.

He picked up the phone to his secretary at the University. "Michael, book me two flights to Australia, destination Ayers Rock ... yes, that's right, I'm taking a vacation ... thank you ... yes, it has been a long time ... as soon as possible."

Borghese redialled, "Meir, you're taking a trip with me to Australia ... yes, we've located them ... no, I'm afraid it's going to be diplomacy this time ... that's right ... I'd feel better if I had some support ... see you at the airport."

He started to type an email, destination Mutitjulu.

***

Mary was still at the Internet computer when an email arrived in her Inbox. "That was quick, didn't think Bob would be up yet."

Mary opened the email and after a few seconds sucked in through her teeth. "Looks like we are going to meet the person who's been trying to stop us."

Si leaned over Mary's shoulder and read the email. "So, he wants to talk to us before we release any information to the world."

"Perhaps we should wait to hear what he has to say. I'd like to hear him explain how all the loss of life and destruction can be justified!" Mary was starting to feel angry again.

"Well, we've got the meeting with the council in the morning so it'll only mean waiting another day. Then we can decide what to do."

Before they closed down the computer, Mary typed in 'Professor Claudio Borghese'. A search engine displayed a number of hits. She selected one;

Italian Professor, aged 58 years, no family, an ordained priest who turned to academia. An expert in ancient religions and North African languages. Currently working for the Pontificia Università Lateranense, Piazza S.Giovanni in Laterano, 400120 Città del Vaticano.

"So, that's who we are dealing with!" Mary shut down the computer.

Boggabri was just setting out the meal when they arrived. The smell of the Kangaroo meat and Yams made them realise how hungry they felt.

After the meal, Mary and Si cleared away the dishes and Boggabri poured them each a beer. They settled on the verandah and started to discuss the day. Boggabri was aware of some of the events, having been in the council meeting with Wundurra, but her eyes grew wide in amazement as Mary described the discussion they'd had with Lucere.

"I wish I'd been there, but I can't climb rocks any more," said Boggabri. "We have been entrusted with a very important duty, to protect knowledge of 'First People'. I told council, we need to understand what's written before we can decide whether to disclose information. They were wise in many ways that we do not understand. We have to be sure we're ready for their knowledge." Boggabri's caution was tempered with her people's dealings with authority in their past.

"We've got something you might like to see." Mary brought the laptop out, opened it up and started the recording she had taken. Boggabri's eyes widened in amazement. She sat enraptured at the image of Lucere.

"Why can I only hear you?" asked Boggabri.

"Lucere was communicating through our minds, it was amazing, the images, I don't have the words to describe it," explained Mary

They spent the rest of the evening speculating on the knowledge that could be stored in the Library and finally, exhaustion overtook them, and they went to bed.

***

The next morning, Si rose early. Mary slept, recovering from the exertions of the previous day. He showered, dressed and met Boggabri who was eating a breakfast of cereals on the porch. Si poured himself a dish of muesli, added milk and sat down.

"This man coming tomorrow, do you know who he is?" asked Boggabri.

"Not really," said Si. "He works at the Vatican University, but apart from that, we don't know anything else."

"Do you think this to do with Church?" Boggabri was surprised.

"I don't think so," answered Si. "I know they have a reputation for trying to suppress anything that doesn't fit in with their doctrine. But I don't think they'd be involved in the level of violence we've seen, that's all in their past. If they were implicated, it would be devastating for their reputation, which is pretty shaky already with all the Mafia funding rumours, the child abuse scandals of the past and their incredible wealth, when the majority of their congregation comes from the poorest parts of the world."

"I hope you right". Boggabri spotted Mary. "Did you sleep well?".

"Like a log ... I think the excitement of the last few days has caught up with me." Mary sounded upbeat. "How about you Si, what time did you get up?"

"Only about half an hour ago ... yes, I did sleep well, must be the outback air," he smiled at Boggabri.

Mary helped herself to some cereals and joined Boggabri and Si. "What time's the meeting this morning?"

"About ten ... We've got a lot to discuss with you," said Boggabri.

Mary looked at Si.

Boggabri cleared away the breakfast things while Mary and Si watched the changing colours on Ayers Rock from the porch as the sun rose.

"Are you ready for the meeting?" Wundurra's voice surprised them. He had walked over and could still travel silently despite his age.

"A bit apprehensive about the decision the council may have taken," replied Mary.

"The council hasn't made decision. That's for the meeting today. I told of events that had taken place and they wish to discuss the next steps with you," assured Wundurra.

Boggabri stepped onto the porch having heard their voices. "Are we ready?"

They nodded and walked the short distance to the Community Centre in silence, each deep in their own thoughts.

The remainder of the Council were already present when they arrived. Mary and Si sat on the two chairs facing the Council.

Mary set-up the laptop and replayed the recording of Lucere. She then relayed the 'silent' conversation. All of the council members listened intently. When the recording finished one of the council members spoke. "The stories from our dream-time are true. All of these years we have known this great knowledge, without realising what we actually knew."

Wundurra opened the discussion, "tell us what you feel should be done next?"

Mary had been thinking about this for a while. "The city we have discovered is probably the most significant archaeological find that has been made. It will rewrite just about every theory we have on the evolution of humans. It will solve riddles we have struggled with for centuries and that doesn't take into account what we might discover from the knowledge in the Library. We must release this information to the world so our understanding of the past can be corrected."

"If we do this, what will happen next?" enquired Boggabri.

"We'd start a major investigation of the site, document the city and it's many structures, translate the tablets. Your community will be famous, academics from all over the world will want to visit the site. Tourism will be enormous once the site has been thoroughly examined. The Aboriginal people will finally take their rightful place in history." Mary was excited at the prospect of leading a major investigation.

"We have a problem ... we realise importance of this city to history of humans, but what you describe would cause a desecration of our most sacred site. We have protected site for thousands of years. We would lose control of our destiny if what you described were to take place." The head of the council looked concerned.

"But we can't keep it secret!" Mary's frustration was starting to show.

"Is there a way to reveal the discovery without putting your culture in jeopardy?" asked Si.

"That's what we need to decide. The discovery is so important, it needs to be revealed carefully, perhaps in small stages, perhaps without revealing it's location until we can organise a way to manage attention that will result from disclosure." Wundurra was trying to reassure Mary the discovery would not be hidden again.

"It would take more than a lifetime to unravel all of the implications from the site." Mary knew the amount of work that would be required to document and catalogue what had been found so far.

"Pyramids in Egypt were investigated over two hundred years ago and they still finding new information ... why must this site be revealed in a day?" Wundurra had a point. "We would like to suggest establishing a small group of people we can trust who start to investigate the site. We don't disclose location of the site until later. We would like you both to head team."

Uncharacteristically, Mary was silent while she considered the offer. "I'm starting to understand your problem. I can see a way in which we could release the information in stages, the translation of the language, the history of their civilisation, their involvement in many other ancient sites, the information about their constructions. I'm sure we could protect the location for a while if we selected the right people. Maybe some of the team should come from your people?"

"There is one fly in the ointment," interrupted Si. He described the contact they'd had with

Professor Borghese, a brief history of the destructive events and his impending arrival.

"You say he wants to talk about how we release some information. Maybe we have more in common than he thinks. I suggest council include you two as special members when we meet him." The head of the council felt they had reached a satisfactory agreement. "Until he arrives, I suggest you develop plans for team. I know of one or two of my people who are skilled in this area. I'm sure they would like to join the team. Thank you for your understanding. We will help in any way we can."

"What about returning to the site?" asked Mary.

"There'll be plenty of time for that," assured Wundurra.

The council members started to drift back to their duties, giving a few words of encouragement to Mary and Si as they passed.

Chapter Thirty-One

The false prophet

Mary and Si decided to explore Ayers Rock as tourists while they waited for Professor Borghese to arrive the following day, so they drove to the visitor's car park and mingled with the mid-day tourists.

"How do you feel about the discussions with the council?" asked Si.

"I can see their point. I was a bit blinded by the discovery and it's significance to our history, but when I reflect on the discussions, they're right. To release everything quickly could cause enormous disruption as the world attempted to absorb the information. Initially, there'd be a lot of resistance, academics don't like their established ideas challenged. Usually, their first reaction is to try and prove something is wrong rather than try and prove it is right!" Mary knew how discoveries struggled to be accepted, never mind something of this scale.

"What about funding? Do you think you will be able to find anyone to support the team?" Si was being practical.

"That's something I haven't thought about yet. It'll be tricky getting someone to fund the team without disclosing too much about the discovery. The fewer people that know about the site, the safer it will be." Mary realised she had that challenge to come.

"And how do you feel about us?" Si squeezed her hand, uncertain whether he wanted to know the answer.

Mary turned and looked at him. His boyish smile hiding a strong, sensitive man who had shown his ability to handle a crisis. Something he'd need if he was going to get involved with her!

As she looked at him she realised she didn't want to say good-bye, she wanted to spend the rest of her life with him. They had only known each other just over a week, but it was as if it had been years.

"I don't know what I'd do without you, and I don't want to find out. You've become an important part of my life ... do you feel the same?"

"I do feel the same. You've given me a reason to live, rather than exist. Mary Freeman, will you marry me?"

Mary giggled, dragged him off his knee and hugged him. They kissed passionately as tourists walked past, some tutting and others smiling.

The rest of the day was spent wandering around, hand in hand, marvelling at the cave paintings in which they were sure they could spot Orbiane images. They surprised long-tailed Geckos and Thorny Lizards, like miniature pre-historic dinosaurs, who scurried for cover.

After walking all around Ayers Rock, they headed back to Mutitjulu.

Mary decided to check her emails to see if she had any response from Bob, and Si was going to update his boss at NASA. They went over to the Community Centre and logged on. Mary had two emails, one from Bob and one from Borghese. She read the message from Borghese. "He says he will arrive at lunch-time tomorrow. We'll tell Wundurra, should give him plenty of time to organise the Council. Now, let's see what Bob's got to say."

Mary read Bob's response. "He's over the moon that we've found a new site. Apparently my internet vilification has quietened down ... Oh, and the police reckon the fire was started deliberately. Borghese again, no doubt!"

Si checked his emails, a string of office memos, but nothing important. One from his ex-wife, wondering where he was. He realised in his hurry, he hadn't told her he was leaving, so he drafted a quick note to tell her he'd taken a last minute vacation and was currently in Australia. They shut down the computer and headed back to Boggabri's.

Wundurra was talking to Boggabri when they returned.

"Wundurra is going to join us for our meal tonight," she said. "The meal will be ready in about half an hour."

Mary and Si freshened up before joining Boggabri and Wundurra at the table. They related the email from Prof. Borghese and Wundurra agreed to get the Council together for a two o'clock meeting the next day. They discussed the amazing stories and history from the Dreamtime that surrounds Uluru, as the Aboriginal people called Ayers Rock and the Kata Tjuta formation. Even today, no-one was sure how these massive rock structures were formed.

***

The following day, they met Wundurra in the Community Centre to prepare for the meeting with Prof. Borghese. They set up some displays of Uluru and Kata Tjuta around the room and positioned the chairs in a semi-circle with one chair in its centre.

"I've warned our people to look out for the Professor. As soon as he arrives they'll let us know and look after him to make sure he doesn't try and glean too much information from anyone before the meeting." Wundurra wasn't going to take any chances.

Preparations completed, Wundurra offered to take them around the Cultural Centre at Uluru, somewhere they hadn't yet visited. He explained the centre was built from locally-made mud bricks, in the shape of two ancestral snakes, *Kuniya* and *Liru*, whose stories are based at the east, south and west sides of Uluru. The two snakes surrounded a central courtyard where Anangu artists and craftspeople gathered and worked. There were also many displays about the area, the Anangu people and their Dreamtime.

Mary and Si found their visit to the Culture Centre added a whole new dimension to the way they viewed the Aboriginal peoples. Their long history, their suffering at the hands of the first white settlers and their slow recovery as a proud civilisation.

While they were in the centre, Wundurra got a message that Prof. Borghese and his colleague had arrived.

They made their way back to the Community Centre in Mutitjulu and settled down with the rest of the council. At two O-clock, the remaining council members arrived with their guests.

Professor Borghese was a small slim man about sixty years old with a thin, pointed face and a goatee beard, now turning grey. He walked in a confident, almost deprecating way. Wearing a dark grey suit and a crisp white shirt, open at the collar, he looked incongruous against the casual dress of the Council.

He was accompanied by a short stocky man in his forties who Borghese introduced as Meir Shavit.

Prof. Borghese was offered the seat while Shavit stood watchful behind. The professor sat upright and straightened the seams on his trousers. His polished black Italian leather shoes were starting to accumulate the red dust of the outback.

"Welcome to Uluru." Wundurra got straight to the point, "I believe you wish to discuss information gathered by our friends."

"Thank you for giving me this opportunity to explain to you the need for absolute caution in this matter. I represent an organisation that was created some two hundred and fifty years ago to support the true story of the history of man. There have been many false claims made during those times that could have destabilised the faith of people. Our task has been to ensure it does not happen." Professor Borghese spoke with conviction.

"You represent an organisation. Why haven't we heard of organisation?" asked Wundurra.

"By the nature of our task, it is important our identities are secret. I have decided to come here to talk to you as I believe you will understand the need to keep this information from the public. This is the first time in our history we have acknowledged the existence of our group."

"Why do you believe this information should be kept from the public?" enquired Si.

"The information you are trying to release is dangerous and will undermine both accepted science and religion. The destabilising effect this will have may cause many to question their faith, anarchy could result."

"Is your organisation responsible for the obliteration of the Ecuador and Sahara sites, the fire at Durham University?" asked Mary.

"We have some very loyal people who are willing to do whatever is necessary. Sometimes, regrettably, we have to take extreme measures to protect the world." Borghese looked her straight in the eye with a cold stare, Shavit stiffened.

"To protect yourselves more like! What you really mean is that this discovery will shake belief in the Church, or at least any church that lives in the past!" Mary leaned forward in her seat. "It's got nothing to do with protecting people or their faith, it's about protecting out of date organisations who refuse to accept the real truth!"

Si placed a hand on her arm. "You have murdered people and attempted to murder us! Is this the only way? How many people must you kill trying to protect something that can't be protected? The truth cannot be hidden. I'd have thought your own history would have taught you that! You'd still have us believe the world was flat!" Now Si was getting angry.

Shavit slipped his hand inside his jacket.

"Unfortunately, some of the actions we take have casualties, but they die for the greater good." Professor Borghese remained calm.

"The means justify the end! How many times have we heard that throughout history? Usually spoken by madmen!" Mary's voice trembled with suppressed anger.

"Would you like to tell us why you've come here?" Wundurra attempted to re-focus the discussion.

"I expect it is unrealistic to think I can convince you to walk away from this and leave the discovery 'undiscovered'. My proposal is that you release all of the information you have found so far, and access to the site, into my keeping. We will then determine when the time is right to disclose any findings, after of course, we have verified the credibility of the information." Borghese hoped this would be acceptable for their sakes.

"If we don't agree?" queried Wundurra.

"We are a very powerful organisation, we have members in many places of power, in many countries. All of them are committed to our cause. We can make life very uncomfortable," threatened Borghese.

"So if we don't agree to terms, you will ensure we don't get chance to release information to world?" Wundurra wanted Borghese to spell it out.

"I think we understand each other. This is a beautiful part of the world that is very precious to you, it would be a shame if you lost access through some change of view by the government." Borghese was confident he could carry out the threat, Shavit appeared to relax.

"We need time to consider your proposal," said Wundurra, looking at the council members.

"I'm sure you will make the right decision. I will arrange for a team to come here and seal the site, pending further investigations." Borghese was used to getting his way. The power and influence of the Torah Cult had never been successfully challenged. "I plan to return home on the next flight, if you can let me know your response by the time I reach Rome. Should you agree to my terms then a valuable contribution will be made to your council, anonymously, of course."

Chapter Thirty-Two

A response

Wundurra made arrangements for Prof. Borghese and Meir Shavit to return to Connellan Airport. He then returned to the council who were all gathered around a computer screen in the corner. "Has it worked?"

Si turned to Wundurra and smiled. "It's as clear as a bell. It should be perfect."

"OK, let's make a copy, then we can send it. Do you have address?" asked Wundurra.

"Well, I have to say, I haven't had any reason to contact Interpol before, but I'm sure it won't be difficult to find," smiled Si.

After copying the video file made by a camera hidden in the Uluru displays that had been placed around the room, Si completed a contact form on Interpol's website. He described the main events that had happened over the last couple of weeks, attached the video file and pressed send. "Should put the cat amongst the pigeons. The Torah Cult won't be able to intercept the message, so it'll come as a nice surprise."

Before the Council started to disband, Wundurra turned to Mary. "Our discussion yesterday about the next stages, have you thought any more?"

"I do agree we need to release the information slowly. Professor Borghese does have a point when he said the world is not ready. But it doesn't mean to say we hide the truth. I think we can release the information in stages; the discovery of an ancient civilisation, release some of their less challenging writings for examination, get the site dated, and finally, the information about their involvement with humans. It will probably take a few years as each new part is discussed and accepted."

"Have you thought about your part in the process? We would be happy for you to head the team."

"We think someone else should lead the team. I would recommend my colleague at Durham, Professor Bob Cunningham. He's an excellent reputation and is totally trustworthy." Mary looked at Si and smiled. "There are other things we want to give some attention to at the moment."

Wundurra saw the exchange and also smiled, "I understand. Some things in life are more important."

***

Mary glanced out of the aircraft window, watching the west coast of Australia disappear. A sadness crept over her as she thought about the wonderful people she had met. Si sat beside her reading the in-flight magazine. Following the showdown with Borghese, they had booked flights back to the UK to discuss the next steps with Bob.

"Have we made the right decision?" Mary asked. "One part of me would love to examine the Library."

"We'll go back, Wundurra said we can return any time as honoured guests. After all, we're spoken of in their stories," Si smiled. He also felt sad about leaving and felt some apprehension about the next stage in his life.

They had both decided to take a year out of their jobs and tour the world. They also planned to write a book about their adventure. Hopefully, the publishing date would coincide with the release of information from the finds in Australia. They'd even agreed on a title, it was to be called 'Homo intellectus', the scientific name Mary had chosen for the Orbianes.

***

They're arrival at Heathrow was greeted with a cold northerly wind and driving rain. As they passed through the terminal after collecting their cases, Si noticed a headline on the issue of The Times.

'**Secret Cult exposed,
many arrests across Europe.**'

He paid for a copy of the paper and read out the opening paragraphs;

> "In a co-ordinated move across Europe, Interpol and local police forces raided the offices and homes of a number of leading wealthy individuals in Rome, Israel, Cairo, Dallas and Pittsburgh. They had all been implicated in a secret cult, the Torah Cult. The Cult was exposed when Interpol received a copy of a confession from their head, Professor Claudio Borghese.
>
> The Professor was found dead at his home this morning from what Police believe was suicide. Although the Professor worked in a Vatican University, the Roman Catholic Church

> has distanced itself from any involvement. Indeed, in an unprecedented move, the Vatican Authorities allowed the Italian Police to search facilities within the Vatican for further evidence.
>
> These searches uncovered information about a two hundred and fifty year old cult, its members and their activities. These activities included murder, destruction of archaeological sites, the subversion of children's education and many other instances of bribery and corruption within existing world governments. There substantial assets have been seized."

Mary and Si felt a sense of completion. He folded the paper under his arm and together they strolled out of the terminal. They took the Heathrow Express to London, followed by the train to Durham.

Bob was waiting at the station to meet them. He was eager to share the latest news about the Torah Cult. Apparently, the European Governments representing Interpol, had decided to use some of the seized assets to fund the exploration of the site in Australia. Much of the criminal activity of the Cult had fooled Interpol for years, the funding was a reward for all of the crimes that had been solved overnight.

Authors Note

The Asteroid 99942 (Apophis) is real and is predicted to pass within 40,000 kilometres of the earth on Friday 13th April 2029.

Timbuktu is reputed to have had the first University, from at least 1581 AD, but possibly 13th or 14th century. There are thought to be 100,000 manuscripts held in Timbuktu dating from as early as the 12th Century.

We have no real idea where significant leaps in human development began, who built the Pyramids, who created the markings at Nazca in Central South America, who created Gobleki Tepe, etc.

Depending on which scientific source you choose, humans in their current form have been on earth for around 200,000 years.

Again, depending on source, the Aboriginal people may have reached Australia as early as 125,000 years ago.

Acknowledgements

Some of the information in this book can be researched further in 'Fingerprints of the Gods' by Graham Hancock.

Thanks to the Internet for providing information that would have taken years to unearth in any other way, in particular the NASA website and Google Earth.

Thanks also to; Phil Cochran, Sarah Pedder, Tim Keeling and Jon Brettell for their help in crafting the story and to everyone else who gave me advice and encouragement along the way.

Lightning Source UK Ltd.
Milton Keynes UK
UKOW051044131211

183690UK00001B/25/P